The Way I See It

Series by L.B. Tillit

Ozzie-Book 1

Zonta-Book 2

Blake-Book 3

Blake

L.B. Tillit

ISBN: 978-1-7352642-3-3
Published in the United States of America

Dedication

To all who see the world from a different angle.

And to those who embrace them.

Chapter 1
Messed Up

"WHAT WERE YOU THINKING?" My mother's voice made me shudder. She hadn't yelled at me like that since I was a kid. "Coach Miller will be so upset with you!" She paced the small area that we called our living room. She took three long strides one way before she turned and took three strides back again. I was sitting on one of the stools at the small two-seat bar that separated the living room from our tiny kitchen.

"I had to," was all I could answer. How could I explain why I stopped Carlos that morning? I couldn't let him hurt Zonta. *And* I was the only one who was able to stop him. My mother came to a sudden halt and looked directly at me. A strand of her long blond hair fell into her face, so she grabbed it and forced it behind her ear. A second later, she shoved both hands on her hips. I looked away.

I could hear her take a deep breath. She was trying to calm herself down. "Blake. You need to help me understand this!"

The constant sounds from the I-238 Beltway, right outside our balcony window, seemed to help calm my nerves. I let my gaze drift past my mother to watch a red semi-truck pass a minivan.

It was lunchtime, and I was home. I was never home during a school day. This was *not* right. I should be at school. I looked at the clock on the wall and realized that I would miss Business and Finance. "I'm missing my class." I pulled my phone out of my back pocket and saw that I had missed some posts. My back pocket had been vibrating on and off all morning. I hadn't read the posts yet since I knew the kind of trash talk my friends could dish out. I had to be sure I was ready. I wasn't yet, so I shoved it back into my pocket.

My mother dropped her hands and came toward me. She took another breath as she lifted my left arm. EMS had wiped off the blood from the scratches Carlos had carved into my forearm and bandaged them while I was still sitting on the bathroom floor. The girls' bathroom floor at school. Zonta had been surrounded by friends looking out for her. I had just sat there, alone. I had always wanted friends. I thought Carlos was a friend, but I was sure he didn't think I was a friend anymore. Not after I had wrestled him away from hurting Zonta. Not after the police had hauled him off in cuffs. Mom's voice broke into my rundown of that morning. "Blake, you may not be able to wrestle with your arm all scratched up." She patted the bandage gently.

I hadn't thought of that. "I haven't shown Coach Miller yet," I said as a matter of fact. "I'll ask him at practice." Then I frowned. "I'll ask him tomorrow." I would miss practice for the first time since football season was over. Coach Miller and the football coaches always worked around practices for those of us who played both sports. But Coach Miller didn't allow any missed practices once football season was over. He wouldn't be happy about me missing that afternoon. Maybe word would reach him about what was going on.

My mother let go of my arm and patted it. "Well, maybe some good will come out of this. Since you're home, you can watch Penny. She didn't go to school today since she has a bad cold." I didn't even know my sister was home. Mom walked over to the front door, right on the other side of the little kitchen. She grabbed her pocketbook and slung it over her shoulder. "I called my boss and told her I could come in today after all, so I've got to get to work. Please stay right here until I get back. Maybe your principal will call me with an update." She took another breath, this time letting it out slowly. She looked at me. Her eyes bunched together a little and it looked like she was trying not to cry. I knew this meant she was sad. She taught me what *sad* looked like. She taught me what *angry* looked like. She taught me how to act as *normal* as possible. She taught me, so no one would treat me differently. I had to fit in.

But the problem was that no matter what I said or did, I didn't *really* fit in. People put up with me because I was part of their team. In the fall it was football. In the winter it was wrestling. Guys let me hang with them and tag along. I tried to learn to act and talk like they did. Sometimes it worked, since they would laugh. But too many times I was given looks by others, outside the group, who were listening. Looks that told me maybe I wasn't saying the right things. I really blew it last semester in U.S. History, making everyone think I was racist. Emma Tang-Lee still gave me the evil eye every time she walked by me. I hated that, since I had liked her for a long time. I loved how she said what she thought and nobody really messed with her. Making fun of her being Chinese was not my best moment. After that, I had pretty much given up on trying to even talk to her.

Then there was Carlos. He was the only person who really let me hang with him all the time. Of course, half the time he spent telling me to shut up. But still, I was always where there was something going on. My guess was that I would *not* be invited to anything else after what I did to Carlos. I felt a tightness in my chest. I didn't really know what would happen next. But I did know that I would never be allowed to tag along again.

Chapter 2

Penny

It felt weird being at home on a school day. The tightness in my chest still bothered me, so I stood up in the small apartment for a few minutes before I decided that I couldn't just stand there all day waiting. Would the school decide I could come back the next day? Would they suspend me for fighting? Would I still be able to wrestle?

I took a deep breath to loosen the tightness. Mom had taught me that the tightness meant I was anxious. I always had a hard time putting my feelings into words, but that tightness was always a giveaway to my family that something was upsetting me. She taught me to breathe through it. So I did.

As I took another breath, I walked down the short hallway and turned right into my bedroom. Well, it was my brother Kyle's as well. My sister, Penny, shared a bedroom with Mom right across from ours. Our one small bathroom was exactly four more steps down the hall. It pretty much was the only sound buffer between the two rooms.

Kyle was fifteen, only two years younger. He and Penny, who was only eight, had a different dad than I did, but their father was still a father to me. J.D. Hunt was my stepdad's name.

Mom told me that after she had me when she was only eighteen, my real dad didn't want anything to do with us. Mom didn't give me her last name, Long. Instead, she gave me his last name, Dockins, since she never wanted him to forget that he needed to pay child support. And Mr. Cole P. Dockins *did* pay child support since he had some fancy job in Newport. Mom said it was his way to let go of some of his guilt for not helping to raise me. I asked Mom what she meant by *guilt*. She explained that it meant that he did something wrong, and he knew it was wrong.

As I stood in our narrow hallway, I wondered if I was feeling guilt. Was that the anxious feeling in my chest? But I knew I hadn't done anything wrong. I knew I had made the right choice that morning.

"Blake?" Penny cracked open her door. "Are you home?" Her voice was soft and her eyes were squinting. She was still wearing her night T-shirt. It was yellow with pink flowers. Her blond hair was stuck to one side of her face.

"Yes." I stepped back into the hall and squatted down in front of her. "Mom went to work. So it is just you and me."

"Are you sick too?" Her little hands reached out to rest on my shoulder. Her nose was red and dripping. She took her other arm and wiped her nose with her sleeve. One of the pink flowers suddenly looked wet.

"No, I just got in a fight at school, so I'm not allowed to be there right now," I said as a matter of fact. Everything was a matter of fact to me.

Penny noticed the bandage on my arm and let her hand drop to touch the white dressing. Her brown eyes grew wide. "Oh, no! You got into a fight. Are you in big trouble?"

"I don't know yet." I looked at my sister who was the only person in the world who *always* understood me. And I always seemed to understand her. The blond hair reminded me that we at least shared a mother. So there had to be a part of her that was born to understand me. There had been times when I knew Penny and Kyle's dad, J.D. Hunt, also understood me. He had pretty much been my father too until I was ten. Then he suddenly died of a heart attack. Penny didn't remember J.D. since she was only one. But I did. And Kyle did.

Kyle looked just like his dad. J.D. was white, short, and stocky with brown eyes and brown hair. Kyle didn't look like me at all and he always told me he was happy it was that way. With his last name being Long-Hunt and mine Dockins, no one would ever know we were brothers. He told me that I better not tell anyone at Hancock High that we were brothers and I shouldn't talk to him. He said he wanted to be his own man at Hancock High. I wondered what that really meant, but I never asked. Instead, I told him I could follow rules easily and had no problem ignoring him at school. He was a freshman and I had not talked to him once at school that whole year.

"I hope you don't get into big trouble," Penny whispered.

"Me too," I agreed and stood up.

I felt Penny's hand slip into mine. "Where are you going?"

"My room," I answered.

"What are you going to do?"

"Look at flags."

She squeezed my hand and made a squeaking noise. I had learned a long time ago that meant she was excited. "Can I come too?"

I nodded as we walked into my room. At least my sister liked the things that made me different.

Chapter 3
Flags of the World

Penny hopped onto my bed before I could settle onto it myself. She tucked herself tightly against the wall, leaving enough room for me to lay down on my back. We both stared up at the ceiling. Every bit of my side of the room had a flag taped or pinned to it. Kyle's side was full of military posters, mostly about the U.S. Marines. He was already in Hancock High's Marine Corps Junior Reserve Officers Training Corps program. He told me that being part of this MC JROTC program would give him a step ahead of others who enlist after high school. Mom seemed to be happy he had a plan, so I figured it was probably a good thing.

"Show me *Turkey*." Penny always started with a country that had a name that was easy to remember.

"Right there!" I pointed at a red flag with a small white star almost in its center and a white crescent moon off to its left. "But you already know that one."

She giggled. "I like the name."

"Now *you* show me *Japan*." I was testing her. I wondered if she would remember.

"That one's easy!" She pointed at the white flag with a huge red ball in the middle. Well, she liked to call it a ball. That was close enough. I told her it was really a red sun, but she insisted that it was more like a ball. I gave up trying to teach her otherwise after ten attempts. She was stubborn.

Penny and I talked about the flags for at least thirty minutes before she fell asleep again. I flung my covers over her and then looked back up at the flags. I knew them all. I also knew the flags' names and when they were first used as symbols of the countries. Mom told me that I could *never* let my friends know all these details. They would think it was not normal. I would be called a freak. I had to be as normal as possible.

Chapter 4

Posts

My stomach growled and I left Penny in a heap, fast asleep on my bed, as I headed to the kitchen. Nine long strides and I was standing in front of the fridge. I warmed up leftover pizza and plopped down on the couch that took up the whole wall between the kitchen and the balcony. My phone vibrated again. I pulled it out of my back pocket and looked. I couldn't ignore the posts forever.

Owen Hemby was the first to post.

blake took down carlos

Then a flood of responses filled my screen. Some from people I knew, some I did not. But I scrolled through all of them.

nw

way

why

carlos was attacking zonta jones. hot girl he's been hittin on didn't hook up at rager. . . pissed him off

girls bathroom is so not cool

carlos didn't have to be turnt to try to force 53X

messed up

wouldn't want 2 b blake

wrong man to mess with

sux for blake

tbh zonta is lucky blake was there

plz she could have taken him down herself

listen peeps I saw her she was shook up good

omg

where's carlos

hauled his ass off to jail. judge supposed to see him today

bet he'll be out in a few hours

blake better run and hide

where is he?

sent home. Bet he won't set foot in this school

he's on his own

I stopped reading and took another bite of pizza. Would Carlos really be out on the streets so quickly? Would he not get into any trouble? This didn't make sense. Of course, I would go back to school. Why shouldn't I? I decided these guys were just giving their take on the whole thing and they didn't know everything.

My phone vibrated again. I looked at it and saw it was not a post. It was a text. From Ozzie. Hancock High's football star who didn't like me much. There was one thing I knew for sure. He'd never texted me before.

blake r u ok?

I put my pizza down on the narrow coffee table. Did he just ask how I was doing?

yes just a few scratches

At first, I wondered why he was texting me from school. But then I remembered he was still at home recovering from his ACL surgery. He'd be back at school soon.

good. heard what u did. took guts.

I wasn't sure how to respond to that. Was it guts or common sense? So I asked a question instead.

is zonta ok?

I knew he was friends with Zonta. Maybe that was why he was texting.

she called me. she's shook up. family at police station taking out restraining order on carlos

good

Something *was* happening outside this small apartment. It seemed like Zonta would at least be better protected from Carlos.

i'll see u at school wednesday

ttyl

That was it. But that was enough. I suddenly remembered that Ozzie had given me his favorite Cleveland Browns cap when he had decided to end his own life a few months earlier. He had to have been in a way worse place than I was at that minute. I didn't get what pushed him to that dark place. At that moment, I was happy the cap was on his head and not mine. His text showed me that at least Ozzie supported what I did, so he wouldn't leave me alone. At least I hoped not.

Chapter 5

Tuesday

School Bus 27 picked up Kyle and me Tuesday morning, like always. And, like always, Kyle sat in the very back while I took the first open seat toward the front. I was ready to go back to school. Ready for my regular daily pattern. Mom had received word from the principal that I was *not* suspended since I didn't really fight Carlos, I had just held him until help arrived. In fact, they felt I was really a hero.

Mom had smiled when she told me this and Penny had squeezed my hand. Kyle didn't say anything. Maybe to him I didn't exist. I didn't really understand my brother and he didn't explain things to me like Mom and Penny did. He just frowned a lot. But that was nothing new. At that moment I was just happy that I could move on.

The bus, as always, stopped at every block along Hill View Avenue. But one thing was off. Each time a new group climbed the stairs, at least two or three teens would whisper and look at me, and then quickly look away. Even after they passed me, I could hear bits and pieces of gossip. I decided to scoot over next to the window and lean my head against the cold windowpane. I could barely see out of the foggy glass, but I could still count the stop signs at every corner. Once I counted six, I knew we were turning onto 17th Street at the next stop. Only seven more stop signs and two traffic lights along 17th Street before we reached Hancock High.

I got off the bus as fast as I could and headed right into the school caf where I grabbed a free breakfast. I didn't sit down, though. I shoved the cereal bar in my mouth and chugged the milk as I stowed my tray on the return rack. By the time I headed back down the hall toward first period, I was halfway done chomping down an apple.

It felt strange sitting at my desk in first period without Carlos next to me. Mateo Meza-Moya was first to arrive. He had his earbuds in, as always. Normally, he would ignore me, but this time he nodded at me before he took the seat in front of my desk. Mateo had been with us in the bathroom after Carlos's attack on Zonta. He practically guarded Zonta until the medics rolled in. I thought he was going to beat the crap out of me when he first showed up, but Zonta had quickly explained that I had helped her. Still, Mateo didn't trust me. I didn't know what his problem was, and I wasn't about to find out. Instead, I left him alone, since it looked like that was what he wanted.

Mateo and I sat in the room for a good ten minutes in silence before anyone else showed up. As people came through the door, some stared my way while others acted like nothing had happened the day before. Emma Tang-Lee glanced at me briefly and then went right to her seat. I could not read her face at all, but it was the first time she didn't give me the evil eye.

I saw Chastity Shaw pause at the front of the classroom and stare at me for a second. A few months earlier, after I had been labeled a racist, I realized I didn't have a chance with Emma, so I turned my attention to Chastity. She was the hottest girl I knew. Her long, wavy, brown hair was always fixed in different ways. But at least half the time it fell down her white cheeks, leaving an intense contrast that made you look at how pretty she was. She always had on tight clothes and she wore lots of make-up that made her light green eyes punch me in the gut. In a good way. I dared to look at those eyes when I could, but not when she was looking at me. But she'd catch me and tell me to stop staring at her like a freak. It had been bad in the fall when I had obsessed over her. I thought she liked me back, because she would touch me and smile at me. But she didn't. She made it clear to me that she and Owen Hemby were together and I didn't have a chance in hell with her. I had gotten over it and tried not to look at her.

But as Chastity stood there looking at me, I wondered what she was thinking. She quickly turned and walked to her seat. It looked like she wasn't so sure either. I wondered what she and Owen were talking about. Had they talked about me at all? Did they think I was a hero since Owen had texted that I took down Carlos? Did it mean he was on my side? I took a deep breath. There was no way Chastity would tell me any of this, so I needed to stop thinking about it.

Just as I thought class might start, Lilly came through the door and looked right at me. She had these bright green eyes that made me look at her eyes longer than most people. Mostly because they made me think about Brazil's flag. I started to think about the flag with its bright green color and its yellow and blue center. In fact, the flag looked like an eye. Suddenly, I realized Lilly was still looking at me, so I quickly looked away. She was the only one in the class to *not* look away. I hoped she would leave me alone and not say anything. I didn't dare look up to see if she was walking my way, but suddenly I saw some black, leather, combat-like boots reach my desk. I looked up and saw Lilly. I looked away, again.

"Listen, Blake." Lilly's voice was quiet. "Zonta is okay because of what you did." I nodded. "So maybe you're not a total creep." I glanced up at her to read her face. Was she trying to make a joke? I saw her wink at me and smile. It was a joke. She was being kind.

I smiled back. "Thanks."

"Class, let's get started." Ms. Williams was louder than normal. She was getting ready to lecture us. Anytime she had something more to tell us beyond history, I noticed she became louder. I wasn't the only one who noticed since everyone, including Lilly, quickly sat down. Ms. Williams took a deep breath. "We are not going to pretend like yesterday didn't happen." She glanced at me and then let her eyes scan the whole room. "I don't know the legal details of what will happen to Carlos outside of the school, and I won't know until it is made public. However, Hancock High has expelled him for the remainder of the year *and* next year." One person gasped while others whispered *no way* or *omg*. I just sat there listening. I hoped she would explain more. "We have no tolerance for sexual assault at this school." She shook her head, and I could see she was trying to control her anger. "It is a sad day when we think that we can sexually harass one another or assault each other. It is *never* a game, and it is *never* harmless." She wasn't finished. "And I expect that *everyone* here welcomes Zonta when she comes back. I better not hear one negative word against her—"

"Ms. Williams?" I spoke before I realized Ms. Williams might not have been finished talking. I felt the whole class staring at me. Had I messed up again? Was this bad timing?

But Ms. Williams' face softened. "Yes, Blake."

"But what about football? Will Carlos play football next year?"

Ms. Williams took a deep breath and then answered. "Not at Hancock High. I can't tell you where he will go or what he will do, but his Hancock High football career is over."

I felt that tightness in my chest return. Carlos may never play football again. He was really going to be pissed.

Chapter 6

Lunch

As soon as lunch period started, I made sure I got to our normal lunch table first. I thought it was a good idea. This way I wouldn't have to ask if I could sit with the rest of the guys. Gavin Sullivan was our captain of the football team and he always sat at the table with Carlos, Ozzie, and some other guys from the team. We hadn't shifted tables since wrestling started. Most of us were on both teams. Ozzie wasn't, but Gavin, Hunter Burns, and Owen Hemby were. So I expected some of them to show up, as always.

About ten minutes into lunch, I was still by myself at the table. I was also halfway through my chicken tenders. I decided to look around and see if I had missed something. I didn't usually look around the caf, so it was a little weird looking at people. As I scanned the area, Emma walked past me. She stopped a second and looked back at me. I felt my stomach flip and quickly looked away. She hadn't bothered to even look my way for a while. I thought I was over her, but those old familiar feelings returned. I hated that I still liked her. It just made her disgust for me worse. I looked back at her and wasn't surprised that she frowned and quickly moved on to join her friends a few tables away. A few more tables back I spotted my brother, Kyle. He was sitting with his friends who were also all about joining the Marines. For a second, I saw him look at me. But, as I promised, I quickly looked away, so no one would know we were brothers.

It didn't take me long to spot the faces I was looking for. They were all the way on the other side of the caf. I started to stand up and grab my tray, but then I saw Gavin notice me. He shook his head. I knew that meant, "Don't even think about it." A few other faces turned to look at me too, but they quickly looked away and started talking again. Once Gavin saw me sit back down, he turned back to face his friends at their new table. I had done as he asked, and he was pleased. I hoped that meant he was still my friend. But the tightness in my chest returned. I knew better.

I decided to fill the rest of my time taking deep breaths and counting ceiling tiles.

Chapter 7

Business

"Hey, Blake." Emma plopped down next to me during Business and Finance class. My stomach flipped again. My old feelings hit me like a brick. I looked everywhere but at her face. I told myself that she wasn't talking to me because she liked me. Mom had taught me to be careful. Just because a girl talked to me, didn't mean she liked me.

I quietly responded, "Hey."

She shoved a worksheet onto my desk and pulled her desk around so it was up against mine. "So I told the teacher we would do this activity together. Okay?"

I nodded. But I knew she was up to something since she asked the teacher if she could partner with me on an activity. At that moment our job was to come up with a budget, together. Emma hadn't had anything to do with me since we had to work on the First Amendment project last fall. Working through that was hard enough since she thought I was a racist pig, which she pointed out several times. That was the same day that Carlos punched me. I had been so confused, since the words filled with prejudice and stereotyping were statements that I had learned from him.

Emma had told me the next day that I deserved everyone's anger. She had been right. I had felt it. That guilt. Mom had said you felt guilty when you knew you had done something wrong. The problem was that I couldn't do anything about it because I hadn't realized I had screwed up until it was too late. Since I hadn't tried to defend myself, Emma had finally stopped talking about it. To my relief, we had made it through the rest of the project without bringing it up again. Still, she didn't talk to me more than she had to.

That had been three months ago. Why was she suddenly talking to me?

We worked on the budget questions for a few minutes before Emma suddenly asked, "What's their problem?"

I looked up from the worksheet and only saw the top of her head. She was still looking down, writing something. "What do you mean?"

She looked up at me. Her long, straight black hair fell into her face and she shoved it behind her ear with one swoop. I tried to keep eye contact like Mom had taught me, but it lasted two seconds before I looked back down at the worksheet. "The jocks. Your buddies. Your bros. Whatever you call them."

"You mean my friends?" I glanced up for a second. She was still looking at me. I told myself *she doesn't like you . . . she doesn't like you . . . she's just talking.*

She snorted. "Okay, whatever. To be real, I didn't see any friends today. Only assholes." She looked back down at the worksheet, shaking her head. "Don't know why you call them your friends when they treated you like—"

"They are." I cut her off. "They just don't know what to do right now. They don't want to piss off Carlos."

She looked up again with her mouth open. I looked away but then looked back at her wide-open mouth. I frowned. I knew that meant she was surprised. Or was it shocked? In any case, it wasn't good. Her mouth finally closed, and her head tilted. "Are you serious?"

I nodded and looked back down at the worksheet. We hadn't gotten very far. I tried to read the next question for a second time.

But I didn't get past the first word before Emma leaned down, her chin almost touching the paper as she stared up at me. "There is nothing to figure out, you silly frog. They dropped you like a log into a hot fire."

"What do you mean?" I tried to look away, but her face still stared up at me, even as I tried to look at the worksheet. She was so close to me. I hated being so close to people unless it was my choice. I would always pull away or move. But at that moment, I realized I was choosing to let her stay that close to me.

She took her pencil and reached across the paper. "See this?" She pointed at my name that I had written neatly in the top corner of the worksheet, next to hers. I nodded. "This is what they just did to you." She flipped her pencil to the other end and completely erased my name. I could only see a faint shadow.

I didn't say anything. I wanted Emma to be wrong. But I was afraid she was right. It only took one day. One day for the guys I thought were my friends to turn their backs on me.

Chapter 8

Coach Miller

"Not a problem, Blake." Coach Miller placed the bandage back over the scratches on my forearm. "As long as we cover them up and the bandage doesn't come off, then you can still compete."

"Good." I was glad that it was okay.

"As long as you don't have an issue with the holds that will put pressure on those scratches." Coach Miller looked up at me.

"No problem." I meant it.

He scratched his bald head and then crossed both wiry arms across his chest. He was maybe close to 130 lbs. But even at sixty years old, he was all muscles. None of us liked to take him on during practice. Rumor was that he was state champion in his weight class back in the day. None of us doubted it. The old champion cleared his throat before he finally said what was on his mind. "Look, Blake. I heard what happened yesterday."

I dropped my gaze to my coach's feet. I could handle staring at his very worn wrestling shoes. "Yes, Sir."

"You did a good thing." His words were kind, but the heavy weight of the deep breath he took meant he was not finished. "Just watch yourself." I looked up and saw him nod at me. He wanted to say more, but he was never going to say more than he had to. He tried to stay away from his wrestlers' issues outside of wrestling and he *never* chose sides. It was clear that he wasn't going to start at that moment.

Chapter 9
Practice

"Tank. I know you got more in you!" Coach Miller called out as he lay flat on his stomach on the wrestling mat. He was about a foot away from Tank Jee's head. Our one heavyweight, who was sprawled under Owen Hemby, was trying to make an escape. Tank wasn't his real name, but none of us asked him what his Korean name was. Tank fit him best anyway, since he was around 280 lbs. Owen was only a couple of inches taller, but Tank outweighed him by 60 pounds.

"Coach." Tanks' voice sounded so weak. "I . . . I . . . I . . ."

"YOU WHAT?" Owen yelled as he strained to shove Tank's shoulders to the mat for the pin. "YOU WANT TO CALL IT?"

Coach Miller frowned at Tank's huffing and puffing. The rest of the guys on the team started yelling. Some for Owen, others for Tank.

Finally, Tank looked like he was about to give in when he suddenly continued with his statement. "I . . . I . . . need some . . ." Then with one swoop he twisted and made a perfect reversal leaving Owen under his huge mass. Tank quickly pinned Owen and added, ". . . someone who can really challenge me." He jumped up as Owen gasped for air. Everyone started laughing.

Coach Miller shook his head and checked on Owen, who quickly brushed him off saying he was fine. He went up to Tank who was grinning from ear to ear. Within seconds Coach reached him. Tank literally towered over him. Yet, Coach Miller didn't hesitate to tear into him. "Tank. You better think twice about messing around during practice. You think you can just go out there and joke your way to the state tournament?"

Tank dropped his grin. "No, sir." Everyone else was quiet too. Coach turned around and faced the rest of us. "What are you all looking at? Find your partner and hit the mat. If I hear or see anyone joking around, I will personally run laps with you the entire practice tomorrow." None of us wanted that. We had done it once before and the old man had set such a brutal pace. He had shown us we should never mess with him.

"Sorry, Coach." We could barely hear Tank try to make it right. "I thought we could all use a laugh."

Coach spun around and stared up into Tank's face. "You can laugh all you want after the state tournament. But you still have one tri and two tournaments before then." Only when Tank gave a nod and dropped his eyes to the mat, did Coach back off. Tank had gotten the message. Then, at the last second before he walked away, Coach slapped Tank on the back. Hard. Tank smiled. It meant everything was good again.

I tightened my headgear and walked onto the mat. It was only at that moment that I realized that I didn't know who would wrestle with me. I weighed 158 pounds, so I wrestled in the 160 lb weight class. Carlos was my usual partner since he was closest to my weight class. He was only a few inches taller than me and, since he was a few pounds heavier, he wrestled in the 170 lb weight class, the one above mine. He was always the better football player and an amazing running back. But I beat him eight out of ten times on the mat. I realized that I may have wrestled Carlos for the last time last Monday, on the girls' bathroom floor.

I stood alone on the mat for a few seconds before I heard Coach Miller state, "Blake, you will partner with Imani." Any talk between the guys stopped as they all watched Imani walk toward me. Imani Grace was one of three girls that wrestled for Hancock High. Shelly Henry and Nola Lewis were both smaller and mostly wrestled each other. The handful of skinny freshman boys had to wrestle Shelly and Nola once in a while. But they mostly avoided the girls when they could. But all of us between 145 and 160 pounds took turns wrestling

Imani. So this was nothing new. Except that maybe she would be my regular partner now, instead of Carlos. I knew that the silence in the gym meant the other guys were thinking this too.

"Is this a problem?" Imani's soft voice surprised me. She rarely spoke.

She came up close. She was exactly 5'9", just like me. She weighed less and competed in the weight class below mine, but she was all muscle, like me. Her short black hair was cut with three even loops of hair styled against each dark cheek. Her dark brown eyes stared at me as I quickly dropped my eyes from her cheeks to the mat. "Not for me," I answered. "Is it a problem for you?"

"No," Imani answered. She didn't hesitate. Not for one second.

I nodded. And we began.

Chapter 10

Off

I had wrestled Imani more times than I could count, but this time something was wrong. We started from the neutral position, facing each other. We crouched into our stance and waited for Coach to blow the whistle for us to start. As soon as we heard the shrill sound, I went for her legs and took her down. Like always. But then I froze. Suddenly, I had flashbacks to Carlos attacking Zonta. My grip on Imani's legs loosened and I let up on the hard press of my body against hers. Within seconds she made a reversal and had me flipped over and pinned.

"What was that?" Imani asked with a frown as she stood back up for us to start over.

I shook my head. "I don't know." I unbuckled my headgear. I couldn't get rid of the image. I couldn't tell Imani. She would think I was weird. A freak. I shook out my arms and legs and then put my headgear back on. "Okay. Ready."

Imani just nodded. Coach yelled for us to practice escapes. Imani got down on her hands and knees and waited for me. I took a deep breath and came in behind her, placing my left palm on her elbow and reached my other arm around her waist, with my other palm on her navel. The whistle blew and within seconds she moved out of my grip, hitting a stand-up without effort. She turned to face me with both hands on her hips. She looked down at me, since I hadn't moved out of my starting position. "You call that wrestling?" Imani shook her head again.

I looked around the gym and saw the other wrestlers still doing the drill. No one else had escaped yet. I didn't answer her but waited until the drill was over. I knew Coach would have us repeat the drill, but we'd switch positions. Since I wasn't going to answer her, Imani moved in behind me and waited too. I didn't understand why images of the attack were suddenly bothering me. I had helped. I had done a good thing!

As soon as Coach called for a switch, Imani moved in closer, while I got my hands and knees into the bottom position. Her palm on my elbow felt normal, but then she threw her arm around my belly with more force than was allowed. But this was practice, not a match. There was no referee. She tightened her arm. Everyone else was still shaking off the last drill and taking their time making the switch. I didn't like being closed in. I never liked tight spaces. A slow panic began to form. Coach needed to blow the whistle. Soon. Imani tightened her arm even more. I began to breathe harder. Suddenly, the whistle blew and at that moment I didn't think of Zonta or Carlos. I made a forceful escape before Imani knew what had hit her. This time when I turned around Imani was nodding her head. "Okay, that's more like it!"

I didn't smile. I needed to breathe! I didn't wait to see if the others were finished yet or not. I turned away from Imani and headed straight toward the hallway. It was the usual direction we all headed when we wanted some water from the water fountain, just around the corner. But as soon as I turned the corner, I headed toward the door to the outside. I didn't care if I was sweating; I slammed the door open and headed for the closest beam that jutted out like an arch from the side of the gym. I lifted my arms and leaned into the beam, my forehead almost touching the rough wood. I let the cold air soothe my lungs as I breathed deeply.

"What's going on?" Imani must have followed me. "Are you hurt?"

I didn't turn to face her. "Don't do that again," I said as a matter of fact.

I could hear Imani come in close. "Do what?"

"That illegal grip around my waist." I dropped my arms and turned to face her, but I looked at the frozen grass at my feet. "You know it has to be loose. Otherwise, I feel trapped. I *can't* feel trapped. I just can't!"

Imani cleared her throat. "I'll tell you what," she started. I looked at her face for clues to tell me if she was pissed at me or not. Her eyes were wide and her head was tilted. I guessed she was trying to figure me out more than anything. "If you start wrestling me like I'm your equal, then I'll play fair."

I dropped my eyes. "I'm trying, but . . ."

"But what?" I could hear her move in even closer. A cold breeze hit both of us.

I shivered as the memory of Zonta screaming came flooding back, again. "I don't want to hurt you." I suddenly pressed down the tape around my bandage. But I hadn't hurt Zonta. Or had I? I had let Carlos take it too far. Maybe I wasn't a hero. Guilt hit me like a punch in the chest. I took a deep breath.

I looked up to see why Imani had not responded yet and saw her look at my arm, then at me. Her eyes went wide. She knew. I looked away. She cleared her throat again. "You won't." I looked up at her. She added, "But . . . I *might* hurt you."

I frowned. I could see she was trying to tease me. But I couldn't push past the guilt. We could barely hear the whistle blow from inside the gym. We both realized we had missed preparing for the switch to continue practicing the escape. We ran back into the gym, down the hall, and faced Coach as he flung his hands in the air at us. We knew he was giving us his *what-in-the-hell-are-you-doing* look. We both hurried into position, with Imani on the bottom. She jerked forward and I held tight. I was still not my best since she still hit a stand-up before the others. But this time she looked at me and said, "Better."

It wasn't like the images or the sounds of Carlos's attack on Zonta went away. But Imani let me work through it. She didn't say another word that afternoon. She wouldn't let up on me either. She outdid me on almost every drill and when we practiced actual matches, she took me down, pinning me several times. Once in a while, I saw Coach and the other wrestlers stare at us. I knew Coach was worried, but he, too, knew I needed to work it out for myself. At least by the end of practice, I was able to pin Imani a few times.

No one said anything to me during practice. Gavin looked my way a few times and so did Hunter and Owen, but they kept to themselves. They could have teased me about how I had been schooled by Imani. But they didn't. I didn't know what to expect. I didn't want to believe Emma's statement. I didn't want to believe that they had erased me from their group. I simply didn't know. But I did know that I had to come back with my head in a better place. We had a tri-meet Thursday. It would count. I needed to keep my strong wrestling record. I needed to find my way back. Fast!

Chapter 11

Out

After practice, I got on Bus 51 to head home. As always. We only had one car and Mom used it to get to work. Kyle was working on convincing Mom that when he turned sixteen that summer, she should let him use the car and he could drop her off at work. Mom always answered, "We'll see." For the time being, though, anything that caused us to miss riding the school bus home meant that we had to take Bus 51. It never bothered me. Not until that day.

I got on the bus and headed to the first open seat. Just as I was about to sit down, I saw someone sitting at the back of the mostly empty bus. Someone I knew. Carlos. At first I felt myself smile and wave. I *actually* waved before I caught myself. I was so used to being friends. I always smiled and waved at Carlos. But my head quickly caught up with what I was doing. I jerked my hand down and quickly sat in my seat. My back was to Carlos. I knew this was a bad position to be in, leaving myself open to an attack from behind. I quickly shoved my back up against the window of the bus so I could see if Carlos moved my way or not. I went over and over in my head trying to figure out why he was on the bus. He never took Bus 51 after practice, but he knew I did. He knew my pattern.

Before we even pulled out of the bus stop, Carlos moved to the open seat right behind me. It was just him. At least that was good. I could protect myself one on one, but I was stuck when he got others to help him. Like last fall when he and other football players threw some punches at me for being racist. I wished I hadn't said anything that day. I wished I knew when to shut up.

I swallowed and tried to act normal. At least what I thought *normal* should look like. "Hi, Carlos. Looks like you're a free man." I glanced at him and his dark eyes were just staring at me. His jaw was flexing. I took a deep breath. "Some of the guys said they thought you'd get out fast. That's good, right?" I glanced at him again. He was still staring. So I kept talking. "I guess you're not going to be as bad off as—"

"Shut . . . up . . . Blake," Carlos said, slowly. His voice was low and intense. Those three words had come out of his mouth so many times before. But at that moment, it was like I heard them for the first time. Words that controlled me in the past. Words that still controlled me at that moment. I felt my chest tighten. I tried to take a deep breath, but it was hard. He continued, "How could you do this to me? I thought

I could count on you." I looked at my leg that was perched up on the bus seat. I could see my knee through one of the perfectly placed holes in my jeans. When I didn't say anything, Carlos raised his voice. "Are you going to answer me?"

I glanced at his face and then back at my knee. "I didn't do anything to you. I just made sure you didn't hurt Zonta."

He calmly said, "I wasn't hurting her. You know she was having fun."

I frowned. "She was screaming."

"She was playing with me." Cool. Calm and certain. Carlos knew how to mess with me. He knew I believed him. Always.

I shook my head. "No. That's not true."

"Yes, it is."

"No . . . it is not," I said slowly. The calm in my voice surprised me. With one swoop Carlos slapped the top of my head. I jumped up ready to fight.

"Hey! What's going on?" The bus driver's voice boomed. "Sit down or get off at the next stop!"

"Yes, sir! No problems back here! Just messing around." Carlos gave the bus driver his classic smile. The one that had let him get out of trouble his whole life. The one I bet he used on the judge.

The bus driver's eyes kept moving back and forth from the road to his mirror. "You better not mess around on my bus!" I sat back down, forcing myself to keep my eyes on Carlos, or at least his hands.

"Yes, sir." Carlos held that smile until he could see the bus driver had stopped looking.

"Did they let you go because you made them think you were a poor boy who doesn't know better?" I asked, seriously curious.

Carlos turned his smile on me, but it changed into a smirk. "Something like that." His stare returned. My eyes went between his hands and his face. It was not easy, but I wasn't going to have him slap me again. "Here's the thing. I got off easy because it's my first time. They blamed my father for teaching me bad habits and for not being around. So basically my uncle is responsible for me now. Since I'm still a minor, as long as I don't get in trouble, then I'll move past this without many problems." His jaw clenched again. "Except for one *big* problem." He pointed his finger at me. "You and Zonta got me expelled. It doesn't matter what the court says. Zonta has a restraining order out on me and the school won't let me come back. No school, no football. No football, no future."

I frowned. I was trying to figure out why he was telling me this. "So you have to be careful not to get in trouble with the law anymore?" I asked, almost hopeful. He can't hurt Zonta again. He can't hurt me.

Not unless he wanted it all to count and go on his record as an adult. He wasn't that stupid.

Carlos smirked again and stood up as the bus came to a stop. I couldn't believe it was only the first stop. The one where all the teens liked to hang out. "Don't worry, Blake. I won't hurt you. Not physically. But there are so many other ways that I can take you down." He leaned in. "Trust me!"

He jumped off the bus and headed straight for Hancock Burgers. As the bus pulled away, I saw Gavin, Owen, and Hunter waiting for Carlos. They embraced him like a long-lost brother. I took a deep breath. At least he couldn't hurt me, or Zonta. I wasn't sure what he meant about hurting me in other ways, so I gave up trying to figure it out. Instead, I leaned my head against the cool window pane and started to count stop signs.

Chapter 12

Lost

I couldn't get home fast enough. As I walked into my apartment building, I let the door go without looking. It always slammed behind me. It wasn't until I started up the four flights of stairs that I realized that the door took longer to slam than normal. Just as I was about to go back and make sure it had closed, I heard it slam. I decided to keep climbing up the steps. When I reached the second floor, I heard someone else's footsteps. I suddenly worried that Carlos had somehow managed to follow the bus. It didn't make sense, but still, I didn't want to take a chance. I took deep breaths as I picked up my pace.

Just as I reached the fourth floor, I heard the third-floor door open and slam shut. I let out a deep breath. I was worrying about nothing. I needed to chill out.

Suddenly, I heard yelling, which happened a lot in my building. But I was curious. The yelling was coming from the third floor. I stood still and listened.

The third-floor door flew open as the argument moved into the stairwell. "I TOLD YOU TO LEAVE ME ALONE!" a man yelled. I didn't budge. I didn't want them to hear me open the door to my floor and come running up to figure out who was snooping. *No one* in my building liked others getting into their business.

"I don't have anywhere else to go!" a familiar female voice responded. But I couldn't figure out who it was. "She's your mother and YOU need to help her."

I could hear a snort. "She's a drunk!"

"She's *your* mother!" the female responded. I was happy they weren't yelling anymore.

"I've got too much going on," the man explained. "Got three babies of my own and Steph's due with my first son in the summer." Steph. Steph? The name sounded familiar. I knew there was a Steph Pritt that lived on the third floor. She had a little girl around two years old. Mom had told me that she was bad news and to stay clear of her. I never asked why, but I didn't really care. I didn't really talk to many people in the building. In fact, most people who lived in my neighborhood stayed out of each other's business.

"What am I supposed to do? She's drinking away any money she brings home. Can't remember the last time she bought food." The female voice sounded desperate.

"Oh, okay," the man responded. "Here! Take some money and go get some food." When the female didn't respond the man snorted again. "Not even going to thank me? Whatever! Just leave me alone!" And then the third-floor door slammed again.

I grabbed the door handle to finally head onto my own floor when I heard someone start to cry. I told myself that it was none of my business and started to pull the door open. But then I heard the crying turn into sobs. "This can't be happening again!"

"Lilly?" I said her name as soon as I realized who it was.

"Who's there?" The crying instantly stopped. I froze. I didn't want to get into anyone else's business. Why had I said her name out loud? "Hello?" I heard her begin to climb the stairs. Within seconds she was staring up at me from the base of the final set of steps. "Blake?"

I let go of the door handle and waved. "Hi, Lilly."

She wiped her face with the back of her left hand. She was wearing a blue winter jacket and her dirty-blond hair was spilling out from under a red wool cap. Her black, combat-like boots looked a little scuffed up. "What're you doing here?" She was frowning at me. "You shouldn't be here. Are you lost?"

"I live here," I said as a matter of fact.

"You do?" Lilly looked at me. Really looked at me. Her Brazil-flag-green eyes started with my Nike shoes and worked their way up to my black winter jacket with the word *Columbia* standing out in bold white letters.

I shifted. "My mom's great at finding deals." I tried to smile. "No need to scream that we're poor." Mom had always made sure we looked like we could buy the best clothes, even if it was her awesome ability to hit the secondhand stores at the right times. She had us wear brand names so no one would assume we lived in buildings run by Hancock Housing Authority. She didn't want people's first opinions of us to be pity or judgment. So Penny, Kyle, and I wore whatever Mom found. When Kyle was thirteen, he had wished for some new American Eagle jeans and pushed Mom to buy him some. She found some at a secondhand store, washed and ironed them, and attached a fake price tag to the pants. He was so excited. But a week later she told him what she had done, making him feel stupid. He never asked for anything new again.

"Well, she's doing a great job." Lilly nodded. "Okay. So, see you at school." She turned away.

"Wait." I took a step toward the top of the stairs. Lilly looked back up at me. "What're *you* doing here?"

Lilly sighed. "Good question." She looked down at her right hand, which was gripping a twenty-dollar bill.

"Are you okay?" I asked. I knew she'd been crying, so something was wrong.

She smiled. "Yeah. I'm fine."

"But you were crying. Are you hungry?" I frowned. She wasn't making any sense.

"You heard that?" Lilly sighed. "Listen, Blake. It's complicated. Can you just not tell anyone I was here? You know? I got some money now. I'll get me some food." She nodded and then kept nodding. "I promise I'm fine." Her nodding continued as she stared at me. I wasn't sure what she wanted me to say. When I didn't say anything, she stopped nodding and her chin jutted forward. "Well? Promise me you won't say anything?"

I frowned. Who would I tell? "Sure. I won't tell anyone." Lilly nodded again and then quickly took off down the stairs. I really didn't understand that girl. I had too much of my own stuff to figure out. I really didn't care what she was going through. The mess I was in took up all the space in my head.

Chapter 13

One Star

"Which one are you staring at?" Penny jumped up onto my bed. I was stretched out with my hands behind my head and focused on my ceiling. The flags of the world offered me an escape from *my* world. I needed it. Talking to Lilly in the stairwell had been strange, but I quickly tucked it away in the back of my mind.

"Liberia," I answered. I waited for Penny to tilt her head back and see if she could find it.

"There!" She pointed at the flag that looked almost identical to the U.S. flag. Except there was only one large five-point star and the red and white stripes only added up to eleven, not thirteen.

"That's right." I smiled. She was getting better at this game.

She snuggled her head against my shoulder as we both stared up at the strange, yet familiar, flag. "Why do you like this one so much?" she asked.

"What makes you think that?" I asked. I never really thought that I had favorites. They all had something that was interesting.

"Because the last five times I've come in here, that's the flag you're always looking at." She sighed. "So it has to be one you like."

I was quiet for a minute. That explained why she knew which flag was Liberia. I stared at the single white star against the dark-blue background. "I guess I'm like that flag right now."

Penny giggled. "That's silly. You can't *be* like a flag."

"Yes, I can," I said without being worried that Penny would think I was weird. "At first, you think it's the American flag, but then you quickly realize something is not the same. I'm like that. A lot. People think I'm like them, but I'm not quite the same. I'm like that one star sitting there by itself."

Penny reached her hand out and patted my hand. "Now I see it." We both sat there for a few minutes without saying anything.

"Change that." Kyle's voice surprised both Penny and me as we sat up on the bed. Kyle was standing in the doorway, staring at us. He must have listened to the whole conversation.

"What?" I asked.

Kyle walked to his side of the room and threw his bookbag on the floor next to his bed. "Change the way people see you." Kyle sat down on his bed and stared at me. Penny jumped off my bed and hurried over to give Kyle a big hug. The one thing about Penny was that she adored both of us.

"I can't," I said and leaned back onto my pillow again. It was easier to look up at the flags than it was looking at my brother.

"You don't want to," Kyle challenged me. When I didn't answer him, he stood up and walked over to me. Penny leaped onto his back and he held onto her as she giggled. Within seconds two faces were staring down at me. "You need to stand up to the assholes and not let them turn you into an outsider."

I frowned. "What're you talking about?" What had Kyle seen? What did he know that I didn't know?

Kyle pulled Penny off his back and put her out in the hallway. She protested, but he said he needed to talk to me alone. Penny pouted, but she let Kyle close the door in her face. He only took three steps before he stood in front of me again. I was confused. Why was my brother talking to me about this? I thought he didn't want to have anything to do with me at school. This was school stuff. I looked at him and frowned. "What is it? Penny's not going to stay out there very long!"

Kyle shifted and crossed his arms. "I saw you at lunch today. I saw how they all ditched you." He shifted again. "I also heard my friends talk about how Carlos is telling everyone that you set him up to attack

Zonta. You were all into seeing it happen. Carlos also said that you only held him back once you realized you would both get in trouble. He made it sound like you had planned it. That you were really the sick one . . . the pervert."

I sat up. My mouth dropped open and my chest screamed. I actually clutched my T-shirt as I took as many deep breaths as possible. "That's a lie." The words felt so empty. So weak. It was as if the truth had slipped away in one second. When had Carlos started this lie? Is this why everyone was ignoring me?

Kyle's eyes grew wide. "I know that, but they don't!" He stared at me as my heart began to race. "Blake! Are you okay?"

Suddenly, I couldn't get enough air. I started taking in breaths faster and felt myself become dizzy. I broke out in a sweat as I screamed. "I can't breathe!"

The door flung open and Penny came charging in. "What did you do, Kyle?" She jumped up onto my bed and started patting my back. "Breathe in. Breathe out." She was trying to sound like Mom. Penny had seen me go through enough panic attacks that she thought she knew what to do.

"I didn't mean to make him freak out!" Kyle was actually trying to explain himself to Penny, a tiny eight-year-old. "I was just trying to help—"

"Don't just stand there! Call Mom!" Penny faced me again. "Listen to me, Blake. Breathe in. Breathe out."

I tried to focus on Penny's voice, but my pain had never been so bad. I just knew I was going to die. Still, I tried to breathe, but each breath still left me with stabbing pains.

I hadn't heard Kyle leave or come back. I don't know how much time had passed before Kyle handed me a pill and some water. "Blake, Mom said to take this *now*." I didn't argue as I swallowed the pill. I knew it would help me calm down. It had before.

Penny kept talking to me as Kyle finally sat down on his bed. They were waiting for me to breathe normally. Waiting for me to stop clutching my chest. I don't know how long it took, but I finally stopped. The sharp pain in my chest shifted to a dull ache. I would be fine.

"I'm sorry," Kyle said.

Surprised to hear that Kyle even cared, I looked at him. "It's not your fault. It's mine. I should have never been friends with Carlos in the first place."

Chapter 14

Ozzie

Wednesday. It was only Wednesday. It had only been two days since the attack on Zonta. In two days, I had gone from a hero to a creepy coward. I had not only lost Carlos as my friend, but he had managed to turn everyone else against me with his lies.

Mom had told me that I should shake it off since all that counted was the fact that legal action had been taken against Carlos, even if it was weak. And, most importantly, he was expelled. But Mom didn't get it. The posts had turned against me, so I stopped reading them and placed my phone on silent. If everyone believed Carlos's lies, I would be all alone.

The only thing that gave me hope during first period was watching Ozzie, with his fancy knee brace, and his Brown's cap on his head, swing himself into class on his crutches. He saw me and nodded, but then spent the next few minutes fitting himself into his desk and propping up his leg. Zonta was not back yet. I didn't know when she would be back, but I guessed it might take a while.

Lilly walked through the door as soon as the tardy bell rang. She smiled at Ozzie and said something to him. He smiled back and then Lilly headed straight for her seat. As she walked past me, she glanced at me for one second before she quickly looked away. I was always the one to look away first. I thought about how she made me promise not to tell anyone about what I had heard in the stairwell. It looked to me like she wanted to go back to *not* knowing me at all. That was all I needed: one more person who would avoid me.

"Hi, Blake." Emma startled me. She stood next to my desk, with a neon-yellow duffle bag slung across her shoulder.

"Hey," was all I could get out. I didn't look up at her. Instead, I stared at the neon-yellow bag.

I was waiting for her to lecture me and tell me all over again what a creep I was, but instead, she smiled and said, "Heard the stupid rumors." I looked up at her wide-eyed but looked away again. She quickly added, "I didn't believe them for a minute."

I looked up again. "You didn't?"

She raised an eyebrow. "Should I?"

I looked away and shook my head. "No, no, not at all."

"That's what I thought!" she said as I looked up at her. She gave me a huge smile and winked at me. Then she turned and headed for her seat. She had winked at me. Did that mean she liked me? I pushed away the thought. There was no way she meant what she said. There was no way she could like me. At that moment I knew very few people liked me.

I tried not to worry about what lunch would look like, but I couldn't help myself. Would I be alone, again? I took four deep breaths and made myself focus on Ms. Williams and U.S. History.

When it was time for lunch, the caf felt like a completely different place. Like I had never been there before. Like I was new to the school and didn't know where to sit. I stood with my lunch tray, which had fries piled high. Fries and ketchup. That was all I wanted. I looked over at my empty table and then at the other side of the caf where my old friends were already gathering. Then I did something I had never done before. I looked for Kyle. When I spotted my brother, he was looking at me too. He nudged his head toward my old empty table. That was better than trying to sit with the "assholes." At least that was what he told me the night before. He still didn't want me to sit with him, but he was paying attention to what I did. I nodded at him and walked toward the empty table, then settled myself with my back to Gavin and the rest of the guys. I didn't want to see if they were looking at me.

"What's up, Blake?" Ozzie sat down across from me. He thanked some freshman for carrying over his lunch tray and then propped up his leg on the metal seats.

"Not much," I answered, although the words were a complete lie. I dug into my fries as Ozzie took his first bite out of one of his two burgers.

We sat there eating for a few minutes before Ozzie looked over my shoulder and frowned. "Why is Gavin waving at me to go sit over there?" He shook his head. "No way am I going to move again." He took another bite. I didn't say anything but kept eating. Ozzie looked up from his food and over my shoulder again. I knew they were still trying to get his attention. He picked up his phone and read a text that was shot his way. He then looked at me. "What is this? What is Gavin talking about?"

"I don't know." I really didn't know what Gavin was saying to Ozzie. Although, I had a pretty good idea.

"He said they are cutting you off. That I should stay away from you." Ozzie put his burger down. He looked down at his phone again. I could tell he was scrolling through those awful posts for the first time. He started shaking his head and pulled his Browns cap off and then shoved it back on. "What the hell? Do you know what Carlos is saying?" He looked up at me.

The ache in my chest was trying to take over again. I breathed deeply as I dropped my eyes to my fries and nodded. "But it's all a lie."

"Of course it is!" Ozzie was louder than I wanted him to be. I didn't want more attention. "Do Gavin and Hunter and Owen really believe these lies?" Ozzie asked me honestly.

I nodded. "Yes, they think I made Carlos do the things he did."

Ozzie shook his head. "Don't they *know* Carlos?" A second later he added, "Don't they know *you*?" I looked at him, and, for the first time in two days, I felt hope. Ozzie knew I could never be that person. I suddenly wondered if, maybe, Emma was being real too.

"I don't know how to stop the lies," I confided. The ache in my chest lessened a little.

I heard Ozzie suck air through his teeth. "Well, I know one thing for sure. I'm not moving." I looked up at him as he picked up his burger again. "No way is Carlos going to control this school when he's not even here! Not after what he did to Zonta." He took a huge bite and wolfed down both burgers like he was on a mission.

Chapter 15

Tri-Meet

Wrestlers in purple shorts and warm-up jackets moved around the gym in unison. East Newport High was the first team Hancock High would challenge. The Hemby Hawks, all in red, were waiting on the side. We would wrestle them next.

Imani, Shelly, and Nola quickly joined me in the hallway that led into the gym to watch the show of purple. We had to wait for the rest of our team to make our own entrance. We would always burst into the gym as one and quickly move into a planned series of warm-ups. It was quite a display of our skills. Up until that day, I had always been part of the team hype before we left the locker room. But since no one was speaking to me, I had decided to wait in the hall with the girls. As soon as East Newport High was finished, I heard Coach yell at the guys in the locker room to get moving. A minute later we were all doing our own impressive warm-ups, all dressed in a sea of black. As a wrestling team, we transformed into Hancock Thunder, each of us with a white lightning bolt straight down the back of our jackets.

Five minutes later we were all facing the American flag as the Star-Spangled Banner was piped in over the sound system. I stared up at the flag and pretended that I was looking up at my ceiling, at my cut-out of the American flag. My flag was surrounded by the other flags. A sea of colors. I felt my nerves calm some. I was so afraid I would fall apart that I had hardly slept the night before. Mom told me to just do my best, but she didn't understand that I was still trying to find the old me. The me that was a great wrestler.

Mom hadn't been to a meet the whole season. She promised that if I made it into regionals, she'd come. And, of course, if I made it to the state level she'd be there too, *if* she could get time off. I never got upset with her because I knew she was working overtime for all of us to live as "normal" a life as possible. Mom worked so hard, so Kyle and I had picked up weekend jobs at Food Time Grocery off of 10th street to earn any spending money. It seemed all teens had random cash tucked in their pockets to buy a soda or burger. It wasn't random money to us. Mom wouldn't allow us to work during the week. School came first. Still, that day in the gym, as I looked at the parents and grandparents who were filling the stands, I felt something was missing.

"You good?" Imani pulled me out of my thoughts. I was still standing facing the flag. Everyone else had begun to move around.

Some stretched, others talked to each other as the referee began the first match in the 106 lb weight class.

I nodded and quickly found a seat and made sure I was ready when my weight class was called. I checked my headgear and then made sure my bandage on my left forearm, across my scratches, was secure. Once I checked everything, I watched our smallest freshman boy, a kid named Adam, step onto the mat. I couldn't tell if he looked paler than usual because of his shiny black singlet, or because he was on edge. He tightened his headgear and shoved his mouth guard into place. He was wiry but fast. In less than fifteen seconds, Adam had pinned the boy in the shiny purple singlet. The other boy jumped up, furious. As soon as he left the mat, he stormed out of the gym. Adam grinned as he walked toward us. His team. After Coach shook his hand and patted his shoulder, Gavin, Hunter, and Owen all slapped his back and told him how great he was. Tank lifted Adam off the ground in a giant bear hug and then quickly put him down. Tank pinched his nose and said, "Boy! You need a shower!" They all laughed.

I focused on each match and scanned East Newport High's team trying to figure out who was in my weight class. They had a few girls. I hoped the one larger girl, with her tightly braided, bright-red hair, was *not* in my weight class. When the 152 lbs weight class was called, my stomach turned as Imani moved to check in. A guy stepped up to challenge her. Not the girl. That meant there was a good chance the redhead would wrestle me.

I began to take off my jacket and shorts to be ready for my match as I watched Imani step onto the mat. As I tightened my headgear, I watched Imani pin her purple opponent in the second period. Again, our whole team cheered her on and then embraced her when she left the mat triumphant. Except Tank didn't dare give her a bear hug.

The referee yelled, "160 lbs." That was my weight class. I patted down the edges of my bandage one more time. I felt myself shudder as the redhead moved into a stance facing me. Before the referee blew the whistle, I saw Imani. She was holding her hand over her mouth. Her eyes were wide. I knew that look. She was worried for me.

Chapter 16

Pinned

The whistle blew. The redhead lowered her level and took me down with a double leg. I hit the mat hard. There was screaming from the sidelines, but all I heard was, "Pin him, Jenna! Pin him!" It was East Newport High's fans, coaches, and Jenna's whole team.

"BLAKE, STAND UP!" Coach Miller's voice reached over the noise. "STAND UP!"

I shoved away Jenna's arms and tried to get my feet on the mat. But she shifted her weight, causing me to scramble forward, not up. The referee blew the whistle. We had moved out of the larger circle, out of bounds. The referee looked at the coach wearing his own purple jacket, who indicated he wanted Jenna to be on the bottom. He was hoping for some easy points, counting on a quick escape.

Jenna placed her hands and knees on the mat. The referee nodded for me to move into the top position, so I knelt behind her. My left palm barely touched her elbow and my right arm looped around her waist for my right palm to rest on her navel. The whistle blew. I tried not to think of Zonta screaming, but the memory came tearing into my head. I froze, again. Just like Jenna's coach hoped, she hit a stand-up and scored on me. A flash of purple then swooped down on top of me, bringing me face down onto the mat. Jenna looped one arm under my armpit and pushed her hand against the back of my neck. She was trying to flip me onto my back. I held myself in place as she struggled to move me off my stomach. My muscles burned as I resisted. The referee came in close and yelled at me to keep wrestling. He thought I was stalling. Couldn't he see I was trying to keep her from pinning me? The screaming continued, but I only heard Coach Miller's voice. "WHAT ARE YOU DOING? MOVE!"

The buzzer went off and Jenna let go. It was only the end of the first period. We had two more to go, and I had not scored on her. As I stood up to move into the bottom position for our second period, I saw my team talking to each other, like I wasn't even on the mat. Except for Imani, who was watching every move I made. Or, in reality, moves I did *not* make.

The second period was worse than the first, and by the time we were ready for the third period I had pretty much given up. She had scored a ton of points on me, so the only way I could win at that point was to pin her. But to pin her meant I had to overpower her.

The yelling let up. It was like everyone knew Jenna would beat me. For our final period, I started on top again. Right before the whistle blew, there was a moment where it was almost quiet. All of a sudden Imani yelled, "SHE IS NOT ZONTA!" I looked at her and she yelled again, "SHE IS *NOT* ZONTA!"

My whole team suddenly stared in my direction. Their mouths dropped. Shelly and Inola pivoted in their seats to get a better look and stopped talking to each other, a feat in itself. Coach Miller looked from Imani to me and his eyes went wide. As Gavin pulled Owen and Hunter's attention back on himself, Tank left them and moved to one side of Imani, while Adam got off his chair and moved to her other side. The contrast between Tank's massive size and Adam's wiry frame looked funny. Another time and place I would have made fun of both of them. But at that moment, the three faces staring at me made me remember I was a wrestler. Part of a team.

The whistle blew and I could only hear, *not Zonta, not Zonta.*

Imani screamed again, "YOU CAN'T BREATHE! REMEMBER? COME ON BLAKE!" The memory of Imani's illegal grip around my waist pushed away the image of Carlos attacking Zonta.

"DON'T LET HER CRUSH THE LIFE OUT OF YOU! MOVE!" Tank yelled for the first time during my match. Suddenly, my muscle memory kicked in and I had Jenna pinned within seconds. She didn't know what hit her.

As I stood on the edge of the mat, Coach patted my shoulder and then shook my hand. But his grip was firm. "Get your head screwed on right and don't scare me like that again!"

"Yes, sir!" I nodded.

As I faced my team, Owen couldn't help himself but start to move my way with a big grin on his face. But Gavin grabbed him, said something, and pulled him back to where he was standing with Hunter. After that, none of them looked my way again. But I didn't care. Imani was grinning from ear to ear and Tank had his arms wide open. He embraced me as I stepped off the mat and Adam gave me a fist bump. Tank laughed. "*That's* what I'm talking about!"

Chapter 17
Forfeit

The rest of the matches against East Newport High played out as always. Some wins and some losses. Hunter and Owen both won their matches with points, and Gavin lost his match. I had never before wished someone would lose on my own team. But that day, I had to force myself not to smile when Gavin jumped up after counting the lights. He was pissed! He shoved Hunter and Owen out of the way as they tried to tell him to shake it off. Tank, our heavyweight, pinned his opponent at the end of the first period. It was expected. Still, we all celebrated. Most of all, Tank celebrated. He made us all laugh as he grabbed his bottle and squirted water all over his face like he had just won the hardest match of his life. Coach was really trying not to smile, but he couldn't help shaking his head and hiding a little smirk.

After a ten-minute break and cleaning off the mat, it was time for the second round of matches. This time against Hemby. I didn't want to go through the same screw-up that almost caused me to lose the match against Jenna. Imani hadn't said anything to me since she had helped me get Zonta out of my head, but Imani had never been one to talk much. I was thankful.

Adam lost to Hemby, but he didn't lose his temper when he left the mat, and neither did Shelly nor Inola. Hemby was a tough team. Imani had to fight through all three periods to score enough points. Even though she won, she was disappointed she didn't pin the guy. As she took off her headgear, she said to herself, "I'll pin him next time." I had no doubt she would.

I had my headgear on and mouth guard in as I checked in for my match. But I was the only one to step onto the mat. Hemby had no one wrestling in my weight class. The referee held up my arm and declared me winner by forfeit. They were the easiest points added to the team total.

I hated that I was relieved, but I was. I knew I would have to take on a lot more opponents at the conference tournament. I had a little over a week to get my head in a better place. The last four days had taught me that a lot could happen in a week.

Chapter 18

Stew

"Jerry needs you!" Stew's gruff voice shocked me at first. I almost dropped the last can of Mini Millie corn that I was placing on the shelf. Mini Millie was Food Time Grocery's store brand. Almost every product had a Mini Millie version.

I glanced at my boss and frowned. "But you told me to stock the shelves today." I wasn't arguing. I just didn't understand. When I didn't have a wrestling match, I always came in on Saturdays and Sundays to stock the shelves at Food Time Grocery.

Stew ran his hand through his curly black hair. His gut hung over his belt stretching out the words on the front of his shirt. We all wore the same green shirts with bold yellow letters that read *Having a good time at Food-Time Grocery?* "Listen, Blake, I know what I told you, but I really need you to do something else today." He reached and grabbed the can of corn that was still in my hand. "I'll finish stocking the corn and you can do the rest of this aisle tomorrow. Right now, I need you to help Jerry. You'll find him in the break room."

I stood for a second with my hand still open, watching him shove the can onto the shelf to complete the row of corn. At least five other boxes with *Mini Millie* written in bold letters were stacked at my feet ready for me. "But then I'll be behind tomorrow?"

"No, you won't. I'll have Kyle finish the boxes you already have out here and then he can help you some tomorrow too."

Great! All I needed was my brother doing my job and then helping me. I knew he wouldn't be too happy either. "I don't think that's a good idea." I stated the obvious.

Stew pulled up his pants and tucked in his shirt a little tighter. That usually meant he was trying to stay calm. I wasn't sure why he would be upset with me. "Listen, Blake! I'm the boss, right?"

"Yes."

"So go see Jerry NOW before I decide that you never stock another shelf!" A shade of red was slowly creeping up his very white neck. "DO YOU UNDERSTAND?"

"Yes, sir." I quickly dropped my eyes and headed to the back of the store. I didn't dare ask Stew why he was so upset. What in the world could he possibly need me to do?

Chapter 19

Last Minute

"You got your fancy shirt in your locker?" Jerry asked me as soon as I showed up in the break room. It was a simple room with about twenty lockers lining the walls and a simple plastic table in the middle. But there were only two plastic stools around the table since Stew wanted to make sure we never hung out. Jerry looked exactly like Stew, except he was not as heavy as his twin brother. Stew's name was really Terry, but he hated everyone mixing up *Jerry* and *Terry*, so he took their last name Stewart and shortened it to Stew. I stared at Jerry and wondered why he was not wearing the green shirt like the rest of us. He was wearing a pair of black dress pants and a white, button-up dress shirt with a stiff collar.

"What fancy shirt?" I was confused.

Jerry slung a blue tie around his neck. "Whatever that shirt was you wore today. It will work."

"But I have to wear this shirt when I'm working. Stew said—"

"Stew *said* you need to help me today. So put on your fancy shirt and grab a tie." He finished twisting his tie into a simple knot. I looked at three other ties hanging on the wall. Then I remembered that Jerry and Stew also catered food sometimes. It was more like providing a food truck at ball games and outdoor events. Jerry's hot dogs with greasy chili piled high were Hancock's Little League's favorite.

"Do you have a catering job right now?" I asked.

Jerry rolled his eyes. "I thought Stew told you! Listen, Blake, someone needs some last-minute appetizers for an important client coming into town. Looks like the upscale caterers couldn't do it, but Stew said yes. Of course."

I grabbed my button-up shirt that was white with a small blue print on it. Another one of Mom's classic finds. With the khaki pants we had to wear for work, it looked professional enough. Jerry grabbed the last blue tie off the wall and had it tied and ready for me by the time I buttoned up my shirt. He flung the tie over my neck and pushed the knot up so tight I thought it would strangle me. I had to grab it and loosen it some.

Fifteen minutes later we were on the road with some deli platters fastened down in the back and several boxes of crackers. "Where are we going?" I asked as Jerry made a right off of 10th Street onto Park Avenue. We were headed toward the center of Hancock.

"Tang-Lee Fabrics. Some big client is coming in two days early," Jerry said as if he catered big clients all the time. I wasn't so sure deli meats and crackers would be enough, but Jerry didn't seem to worry.

The name was familiar. Tang-Lee Fabrics. Tang-Lee. "Wait a second. Is this Emma Tang-Lee's family?" I asked. I felt my chest tighten. As long as I could separate my two worlds, I was fine. At work, I didn't have to think about anything else than stocking shelves.

"I have no idea," Jerry said as we passed Old Town Park on our right. "You know the Tang-Lees?"

"No," I answered a little too quickly. "I mean Emma goes to my school. That's all." I took several deep breaths and started counting stop signs. I remembered how close she moved to me during Business and Finance. I hated that my old feelings for her wouldn't go away. I had too much to worry about to be thinking about her at all. I reminded myself again that she didn't like me anyway. So why should I worry about talking to Emma? How bad could it be?

Chapter 20

Help

Jerry pulled the food truck up to an old building that had a modern look on the bottom floor and a huge window with "Tang-Lee Fabrics" written in some fancy lettering. But the second and third floors of the building showed its age. The faded red brick covered both floors, but the three windows on each floor had some white molding around the ledges. At least it might have been white at some point. An Asian lady came running out to meet us with a huge smile on her face. She was followed by Emma and someone else that I guessed was Emma's brother.

"Thank you so much!" Mrs. Tang-Lee shook Jerry's hand while I waited inside the truck. "My children, Joseph and Emma, will help you unload and show you where to put everything. My clients will be here in half an hour."

"No problem." Jerry hurried to the back of the truck. He banged on the truck's large back doors and yelled, "Blake, I could use a hand here!"

I jumped up and moved to the inside of the truck from my seat. I unlatched the doors and pushed them open. As soon as Emma saw me, she smiled and said, "Blake. What're you doing here?"

"I work for Stew and Jerry," I answered, but I avoided making eye contact.

Jerry's head tilted sideways. "I thought you said you didn't know any Tang-Lees?"

I felt my face warm. "I lied." I didn't know what else to say.

Everyone broke out into laughter. Even Joseph. Emma's brother added, "I don't blame you. I wouldn't claim to know Emma either."

"Shut up, Joe!" Emma gave her brother an intense look. I couldn't tell if she was teasing him or if she was really mad. From the way Joseph frowned, I thought maybe Joseph was wondering the same thing.

"I didn't mean *that*!" My face felt even warmer than before. The last thing I wanted was for Emma to think I didn't like her.

Emma smiled. "Of course, you didn't! My brother is just being a jerk."

"Alright, alright. We better get moving or else your mother won't be happy." Jerry grabbed all the crackers while I handed Joseph and Emma two different deli trays. I opened the small fridge on the truck and grabbed two smaller trays. They looked like several different types of Mini Millie cheesecake. Jerry must have raided the freezer section of the store that morning and thawed them. Out of the package, you couldn't tell the difference between the store brand and other brands.

We walked right to the back of the store and then headed up some stairs to the second floor to a small kitchen. Joseph and Jerry headed back downstairs, leaving me to help Emma. My stomach flipped again. I had never been alone with Emma before. I shook off that thought. I was working. I had to keep focused on the job. Emma grabbed several nice platters out of the cabinets so she could transfer the food we brought onto them. She did a good job making it all look really tasty. "You really make me want to eat the deli meat." I suddenly felt stupid. I should have just told her she was doing a good job.

Emma looked up at me and laughed. "I guess that's a compliment."

I smiled, relieved. "I guess it is." Emma was being nice to me. Maybe talking to her outside of school wasn't so bad. Maybe she could forgive me for all the awful things I said. Maybe she could like . . .

"What's your deal?" Emma asked as she opened a box of crackers, breaking my positive thoughts into pieces. She began to place the crackers in a perfect circle on a plate with silver swirls.

I frowned. "What do you mean?"

She didn't look up at me. Her black hair was pulled out of her face by two high, small ponytails, like small horns. They held enough hair back to show her face but then spilled down her back with the rest of her hair. "What's your deal? You know? Are you special or something?" She glanced at me for a second and then looked away again to gently place another cracker.

I felt my chest tighten and I took a step back. "What do you mean by *special*?"

Emma put down the empty cracker box and turned to face me. Her hand was on her hip and she cocked her head to the side. "Seriously?" The Emma I knew from school was suddenly back. She scared me. She clearly didn't like me at all.

I took another step back and was almost in the doorway. "I don't know what you mean."

"You know *exactly* what I mean." She just stood there staring at me as I tried to avoid looking directly at her. Mom had said I had to learn to hold eye contact longer. She and Penny were the only ones I could ever hold eye contact with, unless they were stressing me out. At that moment, I tried, but Emma was too hard to look at. Her dark eyes saw right into me. "I think Jerry needs me." I lied.

"No, he doesn't." Emma sighed and looked away. "Here." She grabbed one of the trays and handed it to me. "Right now, *I* need you. My *dearest* mother needs her youngest child to blend in as a servant. There's no way I'm doing this alone!" I held the tray with both hands and took two deep breaths. She was done messing with me. I hoped she never asked me that question again because she was right. As always. I knew *exactly* what she meant.

Chapter 21
Clients

I followed Emma downstairs. I made a few more trips up the stairs by myself to bring down the rest of the food while Emma helped Joseph and Jerry finish setting up the table and lining up the platters in some exact order. I could see Mr. and Mrs. Tang-Lee through the storefront windows greeting four people dressed in suits. "Just in time," Joseph whispered as he went to open the front door. Emma rolled her eyes at her brother before she turned to face us. She lifted one hand to her head and rubbed her temple. As soon as she reached us, she grabbed a small water and chugged it down with some pill. I had no idea where the pill came from and I really didn't think much about it. My mother had headaches a lot, so I guessed that it was the same with Emma.

Once she tossed the half-empty bottle in a box under the table, Emma placed me between Jerry and her. We stood in a neat row, trying to look as professional as possible. I was glad she was done talking to me. I needed to move on.

Thankful for something else to think about, I decided to focus on these "big clients." I watched three women and one man walk through the door. Their laughter was polite and they pointed out how nicely the store was set up. All sorts of fabrics were laid out in creative ways. The three women followed Joseph to several couches, where he proceeded to tell them something that made them laugh. The man, though, made his way to our display of "fine foods." He leaned over the cheesecake. "Who made these?" he asked and looked right up at me.

We both froze. It was like looking in the mirror, except his blond hair was turning a dull grey. "Blake?" The man narrowed his brows.

"Cole P. Dockins?" I finally knew what my birth father looked like. I'd repeated his name a thousand times when I was younger. I wanted to remember who my father was in case he ever decided to show up. But after several years, I thought that I would never meet the man. I had been wrong.

Chapter 22
Cole P. Dockins

The look on Cole P. Dockins's face confused me. I couldn't tell if it meant he was surprised or shocked or embarrassed. Those emotions all looked the same to me. But I didn't really react to him, at least not much. He was a stranger to me, not my father. I couldn't remember the last time I had seen him. Maybe when I was four? But it wasn't a clear memory of him.

"Blake, you look good." Cole shifted as he looked at Emma and then at Jerry, who were both staring at the two of us. "Blake is my son." He must have thought it was important to clarify why he was talking to me. The statement, though, made Jerry and Emma's eyes widen even more. Cole looked at Jerry and asked, "Does he work for you?"

Jerry nodded. "Yes, sir. Blake is one of our best weekend employees. That is, on weekends when he's not wrestling. *And* he's an excellent wrestler."

Cole's eyebrows rose. "Is that so?" He looked again at me. "Hmph. I would have never thought—"

"Mr. Dockins, is everything alright?" Mrs. Tang-Lee came over and glared at Emma like she had done something wrong.

Emma's eyes went wide. She grabbed her head and rubbed it for a second. "Ma," she said a little too sweetly. "This is Blake's *father*."

Mrs. Tang-Lee turned away from Emma and stared at my father. "That is so nice. I didn't know you had a son in Hancock."

My father shifted and he threw on a smile. "Well, it has been a long time. You know how it goes. Young love, unplanned baby. Life goes on."

Mrs. Tang-Lee tried to keep her smile on her face, but she couldn't help but frown a little as she glanced at me for a second. "Oh, okay." She said and then quickly added, "How about we sit over on the couches and Emma can bring you a nice plate of food." She glanced at Emma again and said something to her in Mandarin. Emma didn't say anything back, she just picked up an empty plate and began to fill it with food.

Cole nodded and started to follow Mrs. Tang-Lee, but then stopped and came right back to me. "I got to hand it to you, Son, you look almost normal. I never would have bet on that long shot. Good for you!" He smiled.

"Mini Millie," I said as a matter of fact.

"Excuse me?" Cole was confused.

I pointed at the platter of deserts between us. "You asked me who made the cheesecake." I had no other words for this man who was making me sound like some freak, who, by some fluke, managed to look normal.

I heard Emma burst out laughing. As soon as I looked at her, she covered her mouth and glanced over at her mother's back. But Mrs. Tang-Lee didn't turn around since she was already talking to one of the other suits. Still, Emma's eyes went wide as she looked at my father. Just as she was about to say something, Jerry cleared his throat and jumped in. "Sir, I am sure Blake and Emma mean no offense. We're happy to help you with finding—" Jerry stopped as he saw the man in front of him hold up his hand.

"Fair enough," Cole responded. He looked right at me and smiled. "Looks like you got a little of my wit in you. Not bad." He nodded at me one final time before he turned his back and headed toward the other side of the store. The other suits smiled and pulled him right into their conversation with the Tang-Lees. At that moment, Cole P. Dockins proved he was a stranger, shredding any little bit of hope that I might still have had of ever seeing him as my father.

Chapter 23

Nobody

I waited for Emma to tease me after what Cole had said to me, but she didn't. She moved close to me for a second and reached out her hand to touch my arm, but I pulled away before she could make contact. She held her hand in midair for a moment before she let it drop to her side. After a second, she looked up at me. "I'm sorry he was such an ass, but your comeback was sick! You just made my day!" Then she smiled. She held that smile as I made eye contact with her. For only a moment. But it seemed, at least to me, that the smile was real. Like she meant it.

"Emma?" Mrs. Tang-Lee's voice reminded us that we had a job to do. In a flash, the smile dropped and Emma got busy making plates full of food for the clients. Even though she didn't want to do it, she did a great job serving them. But I decided not to point it out. It seemed like maybe it wouldn't be something she wanted to hear. As we each added different foods to the plates, Emma quietly explained to us that her parents hoped to land some orders for several hotel upgrades in Newport. Although it was nice to know what was happening, it just reminded me how little I knew about Cole P. Dockins.

It didn't take long for each plate to look like we were a professional catering team. Jerry helped Emma carry the plates to the couches where the talk had become more serious. Joseph seemed to be as into the discussion as his parents were. As I watched everything going on, I didn't move to help Emma or Jerry, but neither one of them asked me to help. Soon, the two of them stood near me again.

"Sorry I didn't help you serve . . . like you wanted me to." I felt like I at least needed to say something.

Emma shook her head. "No big deal. I get it. If one of my parents had said the things your dad said, I wouldn't have been as chill as you." She glanced over at the business meeting. "To be real, it seems like I'm always fighting about something. I never seem to have that perfect comeback."

I frowned. I thought maybe she was complimenting me, but I was confused. "I wasn't trying to find a perfect comeback." At least I didn't think I was. It was just the logical thing to say.

Emma shook her head. "Well, it *was* the perfect comeback!"

"Why does it matter?" I asked. I didn't know Emma well enough to understand why it was so important to her that I had put my father in his place. Which I was not sure had *really* happened. But from the way she was talking it seemed it could have looked that way.

Emma glanced up at me as I looked away. "It matters because he was *impressed* with you. He even took credit for your answer, saying you were like him."

"But he's a stranger. I don't care what he thinks." I glanced back at her, but she was already looking at her family across the room.

"Crazy how things work." She stared back up at me. I lifted my eyes to her ponytails on top of her head. She didn't care where I looked as she kept talking. "You get a compliment from a father you never see, and I can't get one positive word from people I live with every day." I didn't know what to say, so I didn't say anything. I looked back at her face and she quickly shrugged her shoulders and smiled. "Oh well, life sucks! But you already know that. Right?"

I suddenly smiled. With all the drama going on in my life, I knew exactly what she meant. "Yes, I do!"

Emma was done talking and began to organize the leftover food into neat piles. It didn't matter if Emma thought that Cole's response was great. I still hoped he would not come talk to me again. He didn't.

Jerry and I took off once it was clear we were no longer needed. I was thankful, and I had never been so happy to stock shelves again. But that day really made me think. I had come a long way since I was a kid, and Cole was right. I seemed "normal." But I was tired of it all. Tired of waiting for someone to figure me out. Then start calling me a freak. Or worse, not want to be my friend anymore. But when I looked at what was really happening, none of Mom's rules were working. I didn't have friends and the ones I thought I had were turning their backs on me. Not because they thought I was "special" or different, but because they thought I was a jerk and pervert. Because they believed Carlos's lies. The people who were *not* my friends thought I was a jerk and a freak because of the things I said or did that I learned from Carlos. So I was really nobody to everybody.

Then there was Emma.

There was something about her that made me think. It seemed that the more she thought that I might be "special," the more she tried to talk to me. I knew she knew something when she held her hand in the air for a second after I didn't let her touch me. But she didn't frown. Instead, she gave me a beautiful smile and went on and on about what she was thinking. It didn't make sense.

I understood rules. I understood that one action caused a reaction. That was what made me a good wrestler. The rules and moves made sense. As long as I did exactly what I learned and did it better than anyone else, then I had the result I worked for. I would win. But outside of wrestling, I wasn't getting the same reaction. Working harder at being one of the guys was not working. I wondered if Mom's rules needed to be broken. Maybe I should tell people. Maybe.

Chapter 24

Food Time Grocery

I never thought I'd be excited to stack the cans. I only had an hour left of work, but it was enough time to get going on what I hadn't been able to finish earlier. Kyle helped me move several boxes of canned beans from the back to aisle 4 before he returned to restocking the milk. He didn't get mad at me at all for the extra work he had to do. I kept waiting for him to say something mean, but he didn't. Since he was being chill, I wondered if I should tell him about my experience at the Tang-Lees'. I decided not to since we didn't really have time. I'd tell him later when I told Mom. That way I would only have to retell the story once.

"I don't have a whole lot of hours to give you right now." Stew was standing at the end of my aisle, close to the cash registers. I turned to see who he was trying to hire.

I saw Lilly standing with her back to me. "I'll take whatever I can get." She shifted from one foot to the other. "I can work days if you need me to."

"Aren't you in school?" Stew asked.

"Well . . . yes . . . but—"

"Not allowed to hire you during school hours unless your parents *and* your school give me permission in writing." Stew shook his head. "Don't ask me to break the law."

Lilly shook her head. "I didn't mean to. I didn't know—"

"Now you do." Stew interrupted. He looked down at a paper. I guessed it was her application. "Looks like you don't have any references. No one who will vouch for you."

"Sir, I just moved here this year, and before that I . . . I . . ." Lilly just stopped talking.

Stew shook his head. "Look. You seem nice enough, but I really don't hire people I can't check out. Too many risks." Stew folded up her application form. "I'm sorry."

"I understand. I'll be fine. Thanks for talking to me." Lilly started nodding that annoying nodding that she did in the stairwell. I knew she wasn't okay in the stairwell, even though she kept telling me she was. She was faking it, again.

"I know her, Stew." I started walking toward them, still holding two cans of beans, one in each hand.

Lilly swung around, and her green eyes grew wide. "Blake?" She was holding her warm red cap in her hands.

Stew smiled. "Looks like she knows you too." Then my boss looked at Lilly again. I knew that look. It was the same look he gave me when he was getting ready to change his mind on what he wanted me to stock. Suddenly he looked at me and asked, "What do you know about Lilly?"

I swallowed. I had to think. Fast. I didn't know much. Lilly frowned. She knew I might just mess this up. "Well, Stew. She's in my U.S. History class, so she's got to be a good student. And . . . and . . . she has nice friends. One of her best friends lives in the Bence neighborhood. I'm pretty sure only good people live there." Lilly dropped her shoulders and shook her head. She didn't quite agree with me. "I mean, some nice people live there—"

"You don't really know her, do you?" Stew sighed. Lilly put her hat on her head. She was getting ready to leave.

"I do know her." I frowned. "Maybe not the way you know people. But I know Lilly. At least the things that matter."

Lilly looked at me. I quickly dropped my eyes to the tile floor. Stew cleared his throat. "Okay, Blake, go on."

I began to swing the two cans of beans back and forth. "I know she's hungry." I glanced at Lilly, who shook her head. I had promised not to tell others. But Stew didn't count. "She needs to work here so she can eat." I looked at Stew, who was frowning, as he turned to watch Lilly drop her head. I lifted the cans of beans up in front of me. "You see, I work here so I can buy the things I want to buy and help Mom out, as well. But I never wonder if I'm going to eat." I took a breath. "Give her enough hours so she can eat. I think that could be a good place to start to see if you can trust her."

Stew was quiet for a few seconds. Lilly was still looking away. He finally asked, "Is this true, Lilly?" Lilly barely glanced at him as she nodded. Stew then unfolded her application form. "Okay. You start tomorrow."

Lilly looked up at my boss. "Really?" She spoke so quietly that I could hardly hear her.

"Yes." Stew smiled. "But if you screw up, I'll blame Blake."

My eyes went wide. "What?"

Stew laughed and slapped my back. Which he knew I hated. "Just kidding. Now go put those beans away before you turn them into mush."

As Stew walked away, Lilly looked at me. "Thanks, Blake."

I nodded and pointed at my boss who was walking toward the back. "You may change your mind once you have to deal with Stew."

Lilly laughed. I smiled. Maybe now she wouldn't ignore me at school.

Chapter 25

For Real

"Zonta's coming back to school tomorrow," Ozzie stated as he sat down at the lunch table. His crutches were gone, but his knee brace made it clear he still had a long way to go.

"That's good," I answered as I stared at the two burgers on Ozzie's tray.

"Hope she'll be okay," Ozzie stated right before he chugged his chocolate milk. I thought for sure his cap would fall off his head, but he reached up and held it on as his head tilted all the way back.

"Me too." I hadn't spoken to Zonta since the attack. I didn't even know if she would want to talk to me. I shoved a pea around my tray with my fork. I was grateful Ozzie was sitting with me at lunch, but I knew it was to prove a point to the guys who were ignoring me. I knew Ozzie never really thought of me as his friend. Still, I wouldn't remind him.

Lilly hadn't shown up to school that morning. I had seen her at Food Time Grocery the day before. That Sunday had been busy and Stew seemed happy to have an extra hand. We didn't really talk any, but she looked happy to be there. So I didn't think much about why she was not at school.

"What's up?" Emma plopped down next to me with her lunch box that looked more like a purse. My stomach flipped. Again. Why was she suddenly sitting with us?

Ozzie's eyes widened. Still, he responded, "Not much. You?"

Emma opened her purse-like box and pulled out a yogurt and a spoon. "All good." She tore the lid off the yogurt and spooned a huge glob into her mouth before she looked at us. We were both staring at her. "What? Do you need me to move or something?"

I dropped my eyes back to my peas as Ozzie answered, "Hey, look, it's no big deal." He pointed at the rest of the table. "It's not like we have anyone else coming."

Emma snorted. "That's for sure. Right, Blake?"

I glanced at her and saw she was wearing her hair pulled back in those high ponytails again. "I don't understand." I lied. Emma was acting like we were suddenly close. I liked it, but I was also confused at the same time. I suddenly took a deep breath and put my fork down.

I tried to look at Emma, but her stare always made me look away. "Okay, okay. I do understand."

Ozzie quickly jumped in. "Man, we all get it." He pointed his fork at the tables across the caf. "They're all idiots and like to spread lies."

Emma nodded. "For sure!" She gave me that huge smile and winked at me. Like we had a secret. Did we have a secret?

All I could do was nod along before I started shoving the pea around again. All three of us were quiet. I could hear Emma opening up a fruit cup and Ozzie cutting his meatloaf. I don't know how long it was, but I could feel the pain in my chest begin. A dull ache was beginning to rise. I took two deep breaths before I glanced up and realized both Ozzie and Emma had stopped eating and were looking at me. "You okay?" Ozzie asked.

I nodded and suddenly blurted out. "I've been told that I have high-functioning autism." I took another deep breath and focused on my peas again.

"For real?" Ozzie asked.

I looked up at him and saw a different look on his face. I was pretty sure he was surprised. But he wasn't frowning, which meant he wasn't upset. So I answered, "For real."

Ozzie nodded. "That makes a lot of sense."

Emma shoved my shoulder. "To be real, I've been told that I'm a low-functioning Tang-Lee." I looked at her confused. Then she smiled. "Get it? I can't do anything as well as my brother. Got to be something wrong with me!"

Ozzie jumped in. "Well, Emma, now we know why you're always so angry."

Emma looked at Ozzie and dropped her smile. "Look here, jock. Don't throw shade at me. We aren't that close, yet!"

Ozzie threw up his hands and tried not to laugh. "Oh, I'm sooo sorry! Please don't hurt me!"

Emma crumpled up her napkin and threw it at Ozzie. "Shut up!"

"What am I missing?" Imani walked over and sat down on the other side of Emma. I had no idea they were friends. At least I thought they had to be friends for Imani to join us.

Emma nodded my way, "Blake here, has finally told us he is *on the spectrum*." That was not what I had said. Those were not my words, although I knew it basically meant I had some level of autism. She was right, but hearing someone else explain it made my chest suddenly hurt. I didn't want Imani to know. I wasn't sure why I told Emma and Ozzie. They would probably tell everyone. I took a deep breath.

"About time." Imani took a sip of her water. "Took long enough."

"What?" I looked at Imani and then looked away as soon as she made eye contact.

"Come on, Blake." Imani was serious. "Most everyone knows something is up, but people don't know what, so they make up all sorts of lies. But now everyone can know the truth. Truth is good."

I shook my head. "I don't know about *everyone.* Not a good idea."

"Sure it is!" Ozzie jumped in. "Come on Blake. Everyone has got to know, then they will finally *get* you."

"Get me?" I took another breath.

"Yeah! Like get why you look away a lot, or why you say the wrong thing at the wrong time. A lot." Ozzie explained.

"Is it that bad?" I wasn't sure how to take all this. Mom would be upset to know I had not fit in as well as she wanted me to.

"Bad?" Imani shook her head. "Bad is not a good word. There is nothing *bad* about it. Just *obvious*. That's all."

"It's only *bad* when people think you're a creep," Emma added.

"But spreading the news adds up to talking to a lot of other people." I glanced at Imani briefly. "I thought you didn't like to talk much."

Imani laughed. "I don't. Unless I got something to say." Then she smirked at me. "Which you should know by now!"

"Blake, it's not like we're going to go and grab random people and tell them," Emma explained. "We'll just share it with some people and let word-of-mouth do the rest."

Ozzie was nodding and agreeing with the girls. "This is your chance. But you got to decide if you're good with us telling others. Your call!"

Imani and Emma looked at me and I glanced between the three of them as they waited for me. They weren't going to tell others unless I told them to. They were honoring my choice. Honoring who I was. That was the first time in my life I had ever had anyone let me make the choice. Take the lead.

They waited.

I felt my breathing calm.

I counted the scratches on the tabletop.

They waited.

I don't know how many minutes passed. But as I felt my breathing return to normal, I looked at all three and smiled. "Okay."

Chapter 26

Who Knows?

"Seriously! You can do better than that!" Imani held me down against the mat. She let up and sat back on her heels. It was hot in the gym, and the sweat on my back caused me to stick to the mat. I didn't even try to sit up. The only good thing at that moment was that Coach let me wrestle without the bandage on my forearm since the scratches were no longer on the edge of bleeding. "Come on. Get up." Imani shoved me with her foot. With a grunt, I forced myself to sit up. "What's up with you?"

I looked around at the other wrestlers, all busy focusing on their moves. Everything felt the same. Gavin, Hunter, and Owen were still ignoring me. I expected that everyone would look at me differently. Didn't everyone know? Did nobody care? "Why is no one saying anything?"

Imani sighed. "You really think everyone knows? Already?"

"Don't they?" I was confused.

Imani laughed out loud. I looked around and saw a few of the guys glance our way. Coach Miller yelled, "Blake, get moving!" He scanned the gym. "Next drill! Escapes."

I jumped up and came in behind Imani. She was already on all fours. We were waiting for the whistle to blow. She turned her head to the side. "Not many people know. It will take time. It's not like we posted it to the school webpage. Besides, I'm not telling those jerks." The whistle blew, and Imani tried to stand up as I tried to keep her down. I made her work for her escape.

When she finally pulled away, I wiped the sweat off my face with the bottom of my shirt. "What do you mean?"

I moved into bottom position as she came in behind me this time. "I mean, they don't deserve to know anything. They'll find out when they find out. I really don't care. And neither should you. You think they'll suddenly want to be best friends? Like hell they will! They're in it for themselves." Something clicked inside of me. It wasn't that I was surprised that the guys were selfish, or that I was kidding myself that they'd ever want to be my friends again. It was the fact that they didn't *deserve* to know. Imani made my news something worthy, something important, something *good*.

The whistle blew, and I moved quickly. I felt my old self begin to return. When I hit a stand-up, Imani tried to keep hold and slam me back down. But I did a reversal and managed to take her down hard. Within seconds she was looking up at me in shock. Then she grinned.

"About time!"

Chapter 27

Bus 51

Ever since Carlos had messed with me on the bus after practice, I always looked at every seat on the bus before I sat down. When I didn't see him, I felt myself relax. That afternoon after practice I did the same thing. It had become a part of my new routine.

There were exactly five other people on the bus. An old couple sat at the very back talking to each other. Also, a young woman and two middle-aged men spread out leaving at least two full rows between each of them. I slid into my usual seat, closer to the front of the bus, and scooted over to the window to rest my head against the cool pane. As always. I gazed through the halfway fogged-up glass as the bus pulled up to the first bus stop. I thought I saw some people I knew. So I took the sleeve of my jacket and wiped the pane a couple of times until I could see through it better. Big mistake!

Carlos was sitting on the bench at the bus stop with a pizza box. Gavin was sitting next to him with his mouth full, while Hunter and Owen were standing behind Carlos, reaching over his shoulder to get their pieces. I didn't understand why they would be eating pizza out in the cold when Pizza World was right behind them. As the bus came to a stop, I felt myself begin to breathe heavily. Were they *all* getting on my bus? I'd be outnumbered.

"Getting on or not?" The bus driver yelled at the four of them, who hadn't bothered to stand up.

"No, sir!" Carlos yelled back. "Just needed a place to eat and keep an eye out for backstabbers!" I could see Carlos and Gavin laughing. But Hunter and Owen frowned at each other before they kept eating their pizza.

The bus driver shook his head and closed the doors as he answered, "Whatever!"

As the bus pulled away, Carlos looked right up at me and pointed as he yelled, "FOUND THE BACKSTABBER!" Then he shot me a bird. He held that middle finger up for so long that I was sure that if the bus driver saw it, he might stop, thinking *he* was the target. But he didn't.

As soon as I jerked my head away from the window, I looked toward the driver. He was shaking his head as he glanced back at me through his huge, overhead mirror. As if we were the only ones on the bus, he yelled, "Don't you let them mess with your head! Never, in my twenty years driving this bus, have I seen a bunch of idiots sitting at a bus stop just so they can yell at someone!" I heard a few comments from two others on the bus, but I was not able to focus on what they were saying. I was taking deep breaths. Again. I was getting tired of this.

By the time we reached my bus stop, I had calmed down. I was also the last one on the bus since the bus's turnaround was at the end of our street. As I started down the steps, I realized the driver had not opened the doors yet. So I turned around and faced him to see what was wrong. The bus driver spoke softly. "Listen, man. You must really threaten them."

I shook my head and looked down to count the steps. Only three. "No, sir. I have not threatened them."

I briefly glanced up as the bus driver shook his head. "That is not what I said. I said you *must* threaten them. That's different." I frowned, trying to understand what he meant. I looked down again as he tried to explain. "I mean, they've got to be afraid of you in some way. No one treats someone else like that if they aren't afraid of them. They have to show you that they're in power, not you. If they already thought you didn't matter then they wouldn't have to prove it. They wouldn't sit out in the cold, wasting their time, waiting for you. They'd leave you alone."

My eyes widened as I looked up at him. He saw that I was beginning to understand what he was saying, although I didn't see how that could be true. "Why would they think that?"

"Son, I have no idea. You got to figure that out." He smiled, and then I felt the doors open behind me.

"Thank you . . ." I looked at his name tag. ". . . Pedro." Then I looked back up at his face and really saw Pedro for the first time. He was a heavyset, middle-aged Hispanic man. He was clean-shaven with hair perfectly combed back from his face.

"You're welcome, son."

"Blake," I quickly added.

Pedro smiled. "You're welcome, Blake."

I'd taken that bus for at least seven years, ever since we moved from the upper end to Hillview Drive. I'd ridden on that bus seven years out of Pedro's twenty years driving it, and that was the first time we had spoken. I hoped it wouldn't be our last.

Chapter 28

Zonta

It was Tuesday morning, and I was headed to first period with my backpack slung across my left shoulder. As I walked through the crowded hallway, I tried not to look at the students I passed. It felt like people were looking at me *more* lately. Was it because of Carlos's lies, or because word was spreading about who I really was? Or was it just all in my head?

I narrowly missed knocking into Chastity as she came out of the girl's bathroom. But I did manage to get a face full of wavy brown hair. "Watch where you're going, perv!" she yelled at me but didn't wait for me to respond. She quickly turned away, flipping her long hair over her shoulder, and headed to her locker. At that point, I decided I needed to pay closer attention to where I was walking.

"Blake." I turned around and was surprised to find Zonta standing in front of me. There were no visible signs of bruises and she looked like she always did: very pretty. The only thing that was different was that she wanted to talk to me.

"Zonta. You're back," I stated. But then I dropped my eyes. I remembered the attack, and suddenly, the guilt for not stopping it earlier hit me.

"Yeah." Zonta cleared her throat, so I looked at her. She tried to smile, but couldn't quite pull it off. "Time to come back."

Someone walked up behind me, causing me to step aside. "Hey, Zonta." Mateo pulled an earbud out of one ear. His long black hair was pulled back neatly into a ponytail.

"Hi, Mateo. What's up?" She still held her half-smile.

"Not much," Mateo answered and then looked at me and then back at her. He turned away but left his earbud hanging down. He walked less than four feet before opening up his locker. I couldn't help but wonder what the deal was with Mateo. It felt like he was lurking around half the time. Most times both earbuds were in his ears, but at other times, like that moment, he let one hang down. I suddenly realized that he was listening. How many times did he pretend he wasn't listening? Suddenly, he caught me staring at him. "WHAT?" He glared at me.

I looked away. "Nothing. Nope. All good." I nodded and took two deep breaths as I glanced back at Mateo. He shook his head and looked into his locker. Still, one earbud was hanging down.

I quickly faced Zonta again. "Blake." Zonta glanced down the hall and saw others staring at us. Then she looked back at me. "I just wanted to thank you . . . you know, with helping me and all?"

"I'm sorry about what happened." I didn't know how else to respond to her thanking me. In fact, it bothered me. There was one big thing missing. "I should have done more *before* the attack—"

"LISTEN." Zonta started to raise her voice. I looked around and saw Emma stop a few feet away, along with others. Ozzie was easing down the hall. Within seconds he would be in earshot too. "YOU have nothing to be sorry about!" Zonta growled. "CARLOS was the one on top of me and YOU pulled him off."

I took a deep breath. "But I—"

"Stop it, Blake!" Zonta was shaking her head. "Carlos is at fault, not you."

"What's going on?" Lilly walked up. "Everyone's staring." She had her camo-green backpack hanging off one shoulder.

Zonta and I glanced at the people around us. Across the hall, I saw Emma put her phone away. Had she been recording? She quickly moved on down the hall toward our classroom. For a moment, she glanced at me and winked. Then she was suddenly gone.

All at once, the hallway grew louder. Lots of students were looking at their phones. How many had recorded our conversation? I saw Mateo was still at his locker. He turned his head to look at me. He didn't say anything. I swallowed. Then he gave me one short nod, put his earbud back in his ear, and turned to head down the hall. I took that as a good sign.

Zonta lowered her voice. "I was just thanking Blake, but it looks like I may have picked the wrong place."

Lilly turned around and looked straight at two girls who were still standing too close. She waved her hand and said, "Shoo!" When the two girls looked at her, she waved again. "I said, shoo. Do I have to get closer? Get out of here!" The girls rolled their eyes but moved on.

Zonta laughed. "Lilly, you're crazy!"

"I've been called worse." Lilly smiled. "You're welcome, by the way."

Zonta leaned in and shoved Lilly gently. "Yes, thanks for chasing them away."

I shifted my backpack to my other shoulder. "We better get to class."

Zonta nodded. "Right." But she didn't move. "Look, Blake, I know you don't always say the right things. But there *were* a couple of times you did call out Carlos. Those times mattered." She smiled.

I didn't know what to say. I *had* called Carols out a few times before, but I'd forgotten.

"Yeah, Blake can be helpful when he wants to be," Lilly said. I looked at her and frowned. She punched my arm which caused me to step away. She smiled and added, "I'm teasing!"

Zonta's eyebrows rose. "Wait! What? What are you talking about? Do you and Blake have some secret?"

Lilly tilted her head. "Yes. Blake helped me get a job at Food Time Grocery."

Zonta smiled. "He did?"

Lilly tilted her head in the other direction. Her eyes settled on me. "Yes. He put in a good word for me."

"I didn't know you wanted to work." Zonta touched Lilly's arm. "I guess some spending money will come in handy."

Lilly kept her eyes on me. That Brazil-flag green seemed more intense than normal. I shifted and looked away. Did she think I was going to say something? I had no idea what she expected me to say. I knew I had told Stew she was hungry, but that didn't mean I'd break my promise not to tell everyone. When Lilly realized that I wasn't going to say a word, she tilted her head toward Zonta again. "Yes, spending money. That's what I need. Spending money."

Ozzie joined us as we walked down the hallway, and Zonta and Lilly filled him in on everything that had just happened. But I didn't really listen. I realized that Lilly was like me in one way. There were things we didn't want others to know about us.

Chapter 29

Slow

The rest of the week went by quickly with no other major drama. Both rumors were spreading. Slowly. It all depended on who was friends with whom.

Zonta's statement had been so intense that I thought for sure it would cause Gavin, Hunter, and Owen to come talk to me. Or at least Hunter and Owen, since they seemed a little less into Carlos's lies than Gavin was. But the reality was that I wasn't sure who had been in the hallway. I had run into Chastity as she came out of the restroom right before Zonta talked to me. Maybe she heard the details. Had she said anything to them? She had to have at least talked to Owen. Or did she really not care? Or worse. Maybe she had told them, but the guys didn't believe a word of what Zonta had said.

I knew Emma's video reached all *her* friends, but I didn't share any friends with her. So those students wouldn't really care. Still, the truth had to spread sometime.

Then there was the second rumor about being on the spectrum. I kept waiting for that to hit the guys. But it moved slowly as well. Mostly because those who knew didn't think they needed to spread it as a rumor.

Still, even though I was still being shut out by my old friends, it didn't seem to matter as much. I was getting used to a new routine.

Both rumors, based on truth, would reach them one day. I began to look forward to how they would react. At that moment, I realized something was changing. I wasn't as afraid anymore. Instead, I was curious.

Chapter 30

Breaking Rules

"Tell me it's not true!" Mom moved between me and the T.V. that was on the wall across from the couch. It was Friday night, and I was watching a cartoon with Penny since I was no longer invited anywhere. Penny seemed happy about it.

"What, Mom?" I stood up, afraid something bad had happened. I looked down at Mom, who was holding her chin up causing her face to lean back a little. If I didn't know my mother better, I would have read that she was challenging me. At least that was what that body language meant. She taught me that. But she never challenged me, so it had to mean something else.

Penny didn't miss a beat and took the remote and turned up the volume.

Mom reached for the remote. "Give me that!" She was angry. She turned it off.

"Moooooom!" Penny whined. "It's my fav—"

"BE QUIET!" Mom shut Penny down. My little sister muffled a cry and ran to her room, slamming the door. Mom didn't go after her but stood her ground in front of me, chin still up.

I frowned. "What's wrong?" I asked again, trying the best I could to read her face. Was she hurt? Had someone died? Was she challenging someone else, and I happened to be the one she was talking to?

"Did you really tell people you have high functioning autism?" Mom stared up at me.

I dropped my eyes quickly. I was right about her chin. But only at that moment did I see that she was challenging *me*. "How did you find out?"

I heard a movement in the kitchen. I looked over and saw Kyle standing on the other side of the small kitchen bar. "I told her. A rumor has been spreading, and I heard about it today." Kyle said. He moved around the bar and tried to touch Mom's shoulder. "Mom, it's not such a big deal."

"Yes, it is!" Mom shook off Kyle's hand. "Blake, why did you tell everyone?"

Mom's voice faded for a second. I had to think. Four days. It took four days for the first bit of information about me to spread. That meant since Zonta told everyone on Tuesday about Carlos, then that bit of gossip should be hitting more people by Saturday. I frowned. But we weren't in school on Saturday. Instead, we'd be at the conference tournament. That wouldn't help me any. "Blake! Do you really have *nothing* to say?" Mom still looked up at me as I was figuring out the logical timing of how long it takes for a rumor to spread.

"Mom, it's all good," I said calmly.

"No, it's not!" She dropped her chin and walked to the balcony's sliding glass door. She looked out over the beltway at the cars zooming by. "We worked so hard so this would *never* have to happen. So people would never treat you differently."

"They always have, Mom," I said as a matter of fact.

"What?" She turned around and faced me again.

"Everyone already thinks I'm a freak or a pervert . . . or . . . a racist." I tried not to think of all those times when people had heard the things I said or did. I was embarrassed. "But none of that is true about me." I thought a second. "I guess I seemed to be awful at times . . . but that was because I said stupid stuff."

"Why did you say those things?" Mom put her hand on her hips.

"Because I thought it was what I was supposed to say because of who my friends were." I sat down on the couch again. One word hit me hard. *Were.*

"But I thought you had good friends?" Mom came to sit down next to me.

Kyle snorted and walked back into the kitchen. I pointed at Kyle. "See, even Kyle knows they were *not* good friends."

Mom covered her mouth. She looked at Kyle, who shook his head and added, "*Not good* hardly describes their sorry butts."

I couldn't believe Kyle was helping me. He had never told me he didn't like my friends. Was that why he didn't want anything to do with me? I always thought it was because I was different. I nodded. "Kyle is right. They won't have anything to do with me since I helped Zonta."

"I'm so sorry, honey." Mom patted my leg. "Still, that was no reason to tell anybody. You could have just switched friends." Kyle snorted again. Mom looked at him. "What, Kyle? You clearly have something to say."

Kyle walked back around to us and plopped down on the floor. "Yes, I do!"

Mom and I waited for him to talk. He was taking his time, which Mom didn't like. "Well?" Mom pushed. "What is it?"

"I'm thinking of the best way to put this." His eyes went between Mom and me a few times before he was ready. "Mom, you got to stop thinking Blake can do this *normal* thing."

"KYLE!" Mom raised her voice.

Kyle held up his hands. "Do you want me to talk or not?" Mom nodded, so Kyle took a deep breath and started again. "You can't expect him to act like everyone else. I can't take it anymore! The two of you pretending you have some secret to keep from the world. My whole life is full of memories of all the times you have gone over a million rules for him to keep so the world won't notice. It's stupid! Big time pointless!"

"Not a million rules!" Mom argued.

"Really?" Kyle shook his head. "Seriously. You have trained him so he doesn't even dare to break rules that could help him be liked."

"Give me one!" Mom crossed her arms and shoved her chin in the air.

"Oh, you just want one?" Kyle held up a finger. "Okay, here's a big one. You have the stupid rule that Blake can't tell anyone about his flags. He knows more about the flags of the world than anyone."

"That is *not* normal and will turn people away," Mom argued back.

"Wrong!" Kyle said. I wasn't sure how to take the back and forth. I had never cared about what Kyle had to say before, but at that moment, he had every bit of my attention.

"Really?" Mom shook her head. "Explain."

Kyle looked at me instead of Mom. "Blake, you should share your genius with others. They will think it's so cool. Everyone I know would get a huge kick out of it!"

Before Mom could say anything, I jumped in. "Really?"

Kyle nodded. "Really." I suddenly felt something inside me shift. I wasn't sure if it was excitement or relief.

"But that's a rule I can't break," I stated. "I already broke one rule. I shouldn't break another one." I looked at Mom, hoping she would stop being so angry. I didn't want to feel guilty. Maybe if I kept all the other rules, then she would be okay with me again.

"You need to break *all* those rules! Because they aren't really rules. They are lines that were drawn to keep you from being yourself." Kyle looked at Mom. "I don't know what was going on when you were young, Mom. I do know that things are different today."

Mom stared at Kyle with her eyes wide open. She had tears falling. "But I'm so afraid."

"We know." Kyle stood up and came to sit on the other side of Mom and put his arms around her shoulders. "But just because you're afraid, doesn't mean Blake has to pay the price. Trust me. He'll be alright."

Chapter 31

Conference

The new-gym smell hit us hard as we walked into Hemby High the next day. The quick bus ride from Hancock to Hemby only took half an hour. Everyone was still trying to wake up for our conference tournament as we walked down the bright red hallway toward our assigned locker room. We each lugged our own black duffle bag with *Hancock Thunder* written in white across the side. Adam and another freshman hauled a cooler with drinks and a box full of snacks. It would be a long day, and most of us hadn't eaten yet. Everyone waited until after weigh-in. No one wanted to wrestle in a higher weight class because of a heavy breakfast.

Hemby High had added a brand-new athletic building to their campus. The matches would be spread out during the day between the old gym and the new one.

"Coach, I think I'm going blind!" Tank yelled.

"What?" Coach stopped and looked back at Tank, who was heading up the rear.

Tank raised his hand to his mouth as he repeated, "I'm going blind!" He then swung his hand out, like a real showman. "All this red everywhere is too much! It's like all you can see is red. My eyes can't take it anymore!" He then flopped onto the floor in a heap. Everyone started laughing.

Coach shook his head and ignored Tank as Gavin and Hunter helped him up off the floor.

"I sure miss the Tank Show!" A familiar voice caused all of us to stop walking. Even Coach. A few more feet down the hall, Carlos was leaning against the wall, wearing a red jacket and shorts. Gavin went right up to him. He waved at Owen and Hunter to join him, which they did, slowly. Tank and the rest of us didn't move. I wasn't sure what was happening. None of it made sense.

"Hi, Carlos." Coach finally went up to his former wrestler. "I heard you transferred to Hemby High. Good to see you back in school."

Carlos nodded at his old coach. "Thanks, Coach Miller. Didn't have much of a choice." At that moment, Carlos shot me an intense look.

I felt an arm shove me forward from behind. "Let's go." It was Tank with Imani right beside him. They got the rest of us moving as Coach stood next to Carlos with Hunter, Gavin, and Owen flanking his side. I couldn't hear what else they were saying as I let Tank and Imani sweep me away. But right before we turned the corner, I saw Coach's face turn to face me. He shook his head and started walking really fast in our direction. He was pissed.

Chapter 32

Legit

"Don't worry about Carlos." Tank's advice surprised me. He had never spoken to me about much at all, much less offered any help.

"Okay . . . thanks," was all I said. We passed through a double door and walked into the old gym wing. We were given one of the old locker rooms while the girls had to change in one of the PE classrooms across the hall. With five teams wrestling that Saturday, the girls' locker rooms were assigned to other teams.

Imani looked at Tank before Shelly, Inola, and she disappeared into the classroom to change. "You got this?" Imani asked.

Tank nodded at her. "I got this."

"Got what?" I asked as Tank and I headed into the locker room.

"You!" Tank fake-punched my arm.

"What are you talking about?" I found the closest bench and pulled my wrestling shoes out of my duffle.

Tank moved in close. "Look, man. I heard about you . . . you know . . . the spectrum stuff and all. And I saw Emma Tang-Lee's video she posted with Zonta going on about Carlos. Imani filled me in on the rest." He looked over his shoulder and then at me again. "I got your back. Okay?"

My eyes widened. Saturday. I was right with my calculations. Both bits of gossip were hitting more people. That was good for me. I actually smiled. "Okay. Thanks." I couldn't believe I had Tank in my corner. I hardly noticed Gavin, Owen, and Hunter coming in to join us. I was getting used to ignoring them.

I wondered what was taking Coach so long to get to our locker room. I thought he was right behind us. Just as I was tying my laces, he came storming into the locker room. He didn't stop and talk to the whole team; instead, he walked right up to me. I looked up at my coach as I tied the last knot on my shoe. "Listen, Blake. Carlos says he's wrestling in your weight class for Hemby."

"What?" I stood up and Tank came in close as well. I felt the other wrestlers move in behind us.

"How is that possible?" Tank asked.

Coach ran his hand over his bald head. "I went to talk to the officials and it's legal."

Tank shook his head. "I thought you couldn't wrestle for another team when you transferred schools? At least not until next season."

Coach nodded. "That's what I thought too. But since he didn't transfer because of athletics, the athletic director could make the call. And since there were no serious legal charges, his being expelled didn't look as bad to Hemby High as it did to Hancock High."

"So he can just jump in and wrestle for Hemby High for the last key tournaments?" Tank asked.

"No, he can't." Coach shook his head. "He can't take his season record with him from Hancock, so he doesn't have enough matches as a Hemby Hawk to go to Regionals or State. Regionals is determined by how individuals are seeded based on the whole year. And State matches are determined by performance at Regionals."

We were all quiet for a few seconds before I asked, "So why wrestle today? Why wrestle only one time for Hemby High when he can't compete any further?"

Coach took a deep breath. "The athletic director said he and Carlos came to an understanding that this one time is a good way to see how he is as a wrestler." Then he added. "But I'm not so sure that's it."

"What do you mean?" I asked.

Tank knocked my arm. "Like Coach said, he's wrestling in your weight class."

"But we haven't had weigh-in yet," I said. Carlos always wrestled in the 170 lb. weight class. He was always heavier than me, even though we always practiced together. He'd have to weigh in below 160 pounds to wrestle in the 160 lb. weight class. He was never good at losing weight. There was just no way he could wrestle in my weight class.

Tank sat down on the bench again and looked up at me. "I can't believe this! If Carlos has lost weight, then you wrestling him will be totally legit."

Chapter 33

Sides

As the rest of the guys in the locker room settled back into getting ready, Coach walked right up to the three guys in the far corner of the locker room. Hunter, Owen, and Gavin were quiet, which was not normal. The rest of us watched as the three stood up to face their coach.

Coach didn't even try to be quiet. "The three of you better screw your heads on straight. Now!"

"Coach." Gavin raised his eyebrows. "We're ready to wrestle! Feeling like winners today!" Hunter and Owen nodded.

"I don't give a damn if you are ready to wrestle or not." Coach's voice seemed to grow louder. "You better decide whose team you're on." When his three wrestlers stared at him with their mouths wide open, Coach held up a finger. "One person on this team deserves more respect than any one of you three. You decide if you show *him* respect or if you continue to make idiots of yourselves." In a flash, Owen's eyes looked my way, but then he pulled his attention back to the scolding.

Coach dropped his hand and shook his head. "I've had enough of this! I can't stand one more practice watching this bull! If you decide wrong tonight, then don't show up next week at practice. And as for you two juniors," he pointed at Hunter and Owen, "sure as hell don't show up next year." He then stared at Gavin. "As for you, senior-football-captain, if you don't climb out of this hole you have crawled into, then don't you bother asking me for *anything* . . . ever. I never want to see your face again." In that one instant, Coach broke his own rules. He never got into our teen drama, and he never took sides. I was learning that breaking rules for the right reason was maybe not so bad.

Chapter 34

Owen

Weigh-in was fast. I was right at 155 lbs. I was shocked to see I had lost three pounds in a week. I hadn't really thought about how I hadn't eaten as much lately. I made a mental check that I needed to eat more, even if I didn't feel like it.

We entered the new gym as the Hancock Thunder and claimed a section on the bleachers where we would hang out, waiting for our weight classes and matches to be called. It would take all day, and there was a lot of downtime. Everyone dug into the cooler with drinks and a box of snacks. I grabbed a banana and had downed half of it as Coach approached. We all looked at him as he shook his head. "Looks like Carlos weighed in at 159 lbs." I had a hard time swallowing the banana piece I was chewing on. "That means he's wrestling in the 160 lb weight class. Blake's weight class."

"But doesn't Hemby already have someone wrestling in that weight class?" Imani asked. "It doesn't make sense they would have Carlos take the place of someone who has earned that spot." She had scooted next to me without me noticing. She held a half-eaten peanut butter sandwich.

"They didn't have anyone," I answered before Coach had a chance. "Remember the Tri? They forfeited, and I won because they had no one."

"That explains why they had no problem letting Carlos wrestle this one time for Hemby." Coach said. He was trying to put all the pieces together.

"Maybe he won't even get a chance to wrestle Blake." Tank's voice boomed from behind me. I hadn't thought of that, but he was right. We were wrestling in eight brackets. We were each seeded, so everyone was placed against very specific wrestlers from other teams, depending on how they ranked. It was likely that Carlos would wrestle someone else in the first period and never make it to the next level, the quarterfinals.

Coach dropped his eyes and was quiet for a minute. Suddenly, Owen moved in next to Coach and then looked at me. I looked away, like always. But not before I saw him look away too. I was waiting for Gavin and Hunter to show up as well, but I saw them eating their food at the end of the bleacher. They were shaking their head at Owen, who was not looking at them at all. So I glanced back at Owen and found him staring at the gym floor. "Blake will be wrestling Carlos in the first round."

"What?" Imani started to raise her voice. "Coach, is that true?"

Coach's jaw clenched as he looked at Owen. "Go on, tell them."

Owen took a deep breath. "Well, Blake is seeded first since he has had a great year. The first in the bracket always wrestles the lowest ranked wrestler. Since Carlos has no record as a Hemby Hawk, he is automatically on the bottom."

Imani handed me her half-eaten sandwich and then jumped from our bleacher down to the gym floor. She got up in Owen's face. "How long have you known this?"

Owen's face turned as red as his hair. "Only a few days." He looked at Coach and begged. "Listen, Coach. I should have said something as soon as I knew. But . . ." He paused and glanced at me for a few seconds, ". . . I'm not as good as Blake is at figuring out who the real jerk is."

Coach put a hand on Owen's shoulder. "That's true!" Owen hung his head. Coach continued. "BUT . . . at least you said something." Coach slapped Owen's back. Hard. Owen looked up, pleased. That hard slap was something we all knew. Everything was good with Coach.

Tank yelled. "He just doesn't want to be called a Hemby Hawk." Some of the other wrestlers in the gym were starting to stare, which is what Tank wanted. It was always what Tank wanted.

Owen, who was used to people giving him crap about having Hemby as his last name, looked around at all the stares and nodded. "Well, that's for sure!"

Coach smiled, and a few other wrestlers laughed. Strangers in the stands went back to whatever they were doing before Tank drew their attention. Some of them even looked like they were snickering. I couldn't laugh, though. I was worried about wrestling Carlos. I had lost some weight, and he would have that advantage. I had to take a few deep breaths. Imani grabbed her sandwich out of my hand after she had climbed back up the bleachers. "What's wrong?"

"I'm freaking out about wrestling Carlos."

It wasn't Imani who responded to me. It was Owen. He had followed Imani up to sit with us. He was on the other side of Imani but leaned forward so he could talk to me. "Don't be." I looked at him for a second before I looked back at the half-eaten banana in my hand. There was no way I could finish it. "Listen, Blake. You've always been the better wrestler. You know it, and he knows it. You threaten him." Wasn't that what my bus driver, Pedro, had said?

"On the mat and off!" Imani added as she blocked Owen's view of me.

"I don't get it?" I put the banana on the bleacher next to me.

Owen stood up, walked over to me, grabbed the nasty banana, and tossed it into the large trash bag a few feet away. Then he sat right where the banana had been. "Look, Blake. He knows you are stronger. You always have been, even when you sucked at football. Then in that one second when you took him down on that bathroom floor . . . well . . . he knew he was screwed. Now he's just too desperate to show he's still on top." I suddenly remembered Owen's post that day when he wrote that I had taken Carlos down. He was impressed. Owen pointed at my chest. "BUT he's counting on you freaking out. That's the only thing he has on you."

"Why are you helping me?" I asked as he leaned back and screwed off the lid of an energy drink.

Owen looked to the far end of the bleachers where Gavin and Hunter still sat alone, looking at their phones. He clearly was not going to join them, and they probably didn't want him to. "I'm tired of pretending to be what everyone else expects me to be. From what I've heard lately from Chastity, you must be pretty tired too." So Chastity had done her part to spread the rumors.

My eyes went wide. "You have autism too?"

Tank and Imani were carefully paying attention. Owen snorted. "No! Worse! I'm a Hemby." Tank and Imani laughed. I didn't really get it. I had been to his house and seen how much everyone looked up to the Hemby family in Hancock. I'd learned in school how they had settled Hemby and Hancock. Shouldn't he be proud? Then there was the fact that he could buy anything he wanted!

"That's not worse," I stated. It made no sense.

Tank, Imani, and Owen stopped laughing, and Owen looked at me. I stared at my hands. "I don't know." He started. "I guess you're right. I can't imagine what it's like to be in your head." That was for sure. But he wasn't finished. "I've spent my whole life with people expecting me to act like a Hemby. Follow those Hemby rules! I have to know how to talk to certain people for the sake of the family. I have to act a certain way too! I can't make them think I'm not like them. But I suck at following all those rules. I keep making wrong choices and embarrassing them. And now, it looks like my choice of friends will bring shame on the Hemby family once again. I just can't seem to get it right."

I started laughing. The three looked at me and shook their heads at me. "What's so funny?" Owen asked.

I took a breath and smiled. "You just gave an almost exact play-by-play of what goes on inside my head."

Chapter 35

The Match

It didn't take long for round one in my weight class to be called. There were two mats set up, so at least the attention would be split between the two matches going on at the same time. As I got up to check in, Imani got up too. "Where are you going?" I asked confused.

"My weight class was called too. I have to head to the old gym." She looked at me and I didn't look away. I was suddenly in shock. I was staring through her. "Blake." She grabbed my arm, which pulled me back.

"You can't," I stated. I hadn't realized until that moment how much I needed her so I could feel like I was alright. She had helped me find my way back. And suddenly she wouldn't be there!

"I have to go."

From several feet away Coach yelled, "Blake. You need to check in. Now!"

I felt Imani's hand squeeze my arm. "You got this! You haven't won the right to be seeded first because you have a friend who stands on the sidelines and cheers." Then she let go and punched my shoulder. Hard. "If that's the case, then that's pretty lame, and you deserve to be taken down." As she turned to go, she smirked. "And . . . I'm not sure I want to be friends with a lame wrestler who needs me to hold his hand." Then she winked and was gone.

"Blake! Move!" Coach yelled again.

I walked over to check in as I tightened my headgear. Imani was right. I knew she was teasing me, but her words were filled with truth. I didn't need her. I never needed her before. In a little less than two weeks, I had drawn all my worth as a wrestler from Imani. But that was not who I really was. Imani was helping me, once again, by trying to point out the logic. I had earned being seeded first. I was that good. I just had to remember it.

I turned to face the mat and felt myself shudder as I saw Carlos waiting for me. He was staring at me. As I walked toward Carlos, the referee walked over to the Hemby Hawk coach to point out something. But those few seconds were all Carlos needed. "I will destroy you. You punk-ass freak. Don't think you will make it past this round. Your wrestling days are over." I felt my chest grow tight and I started breathing heavily. I couldn't have a panic attack. I couldn't forfeit this match. But I couldn't wrestle him either. Carlos moved in close. "Good. that's good. You freak out and show everyone what a wuss you really—"

"Gentlemen." The referee had returned. "Are you ready?"

I wasn't.

Chapter 36

Headgear

"Wait!" Coach's voice stopped the match before it started. "I see my wrestler's headgear is too loose."

The referee nodded for me to go see my coach. All he said was, "Quickly." Then he went up to the scorekeeper for a second and joked about something. They were at the tournament to have a fun-filled Saturday. No stress on their end.

"It's fine," I said to Coach as he grabbed my headgear and pulled me in close.

"I know," he said as he pretended to tighten my headgear, "but you aren't." I didn't respond. "You have beat Carlos more times than not. Take yourself back to one of our practices. Before . . . before . . . you know, everything that happened. Stay there in your head. Nowhere else." He then jiggled my headgear as if checking the fit. "Say it! Nowhere else."

"Nowhere else," I repeated.

"Are you there?" he asked.

I pictured practice just three weeks ago. I had taken Carlos down time after time. He kept jumping up, pissed, and then wanted to do it again. Everyone was cheering us on, both of us. I nodded. "I'm there."

Chapter 37

Control

I took my stance and faced Carlos at the beginning of the match. It wasn't so bad. I focused on his hands, which were lifted up in front of him, and the placement of his feet. He was getting ready to attack. We both were. It was the only part of the match where we made no contact. As soon as the whistle blew, we began to circle, sizing each other up and down. Every few seconds one of us would move in and reach out an arm to grab the other one's neck, only to have the arm knocked away. After a few more seconds, the referee moved in and told us we were stalling and needed to wrestle. As soon as the ref stepped away, Carlos lunged for my right foot and lifted my leg into the air. With one swift move, he jerked me face down onto the mat. To make it harder for him to flip me, I quickly spread myself as flat as possible. I could hear Tank yelling at me to get up. Owen screamed, "Fight him! Come on, Blake. Fight!"

I felt Carlos's body move back and forth across my back. He was not sure which side he should stick with. This had always been a weakness of his. I knew he was going to try to reach one arm under my chest. If he could grab my arm on the other side, he could use his weight to flip me. I knew what I would do next. As soon as I felt his weight shift, I moved with it and rolled him over. Then I quickly flipped myself over so I was on top, facing him. Cheers erupted. I felt myself begin to move into my calm wrestling zone.

This would be easy. I felt a lightness return. I told myself over and over that it was like every other time. I was in control. I could still hear Tank and Owen yelling, cheering me on. I didn't dare look to see if anyone else was standing with Coach. But there were also cheers for Carlos. Even though he was new to the team, he was already considered a Hemby Hawk. The bright red team was known for their intense team spirit. The Hancock Thunder liked to think they had more team spirit, but at that moment, I began to doubt it. How could the Hemby Hawks already treat him like one of their star wrestlers? I forced myself to push the thought away. I couldn't go there. Not yet.

Suddenly, I felt Carlos's hand reach up as if he was trying to shove my head away. But at least one of his fingers worked its way under the strap between my chin and ear. I felt the whole chin strap begin to shift. The whistle blew, and the ref called a penalty point against

Carlos. As we both stood up, I could see Carlos's grin. It was exactly what he wanted. I almost had him pinned, but he played dirty to get out of it. I took a deep breath. I had to focus.

I looked away from Carlos to where Coach stood, shaking his head. He walked up to meet me at the edge of the mat. As he checked my headgear, for real that time, he quickly said, "Don't let him get the upper hand. It's still your match. Your win." As I nodded at Coach, I noticed that Tank and Owen were not standing alone. Adam and several others had come in to watch as well. Then I turned to face Carlos again. Avoiding Carlos's smirk as I walked toward him, I scanned the bleachers and spotted Gavin and Hunter watching. They were not cheering. Not yelling at all. But still, they were taking in every move.

Chapter 38

Messed Up

The referee had us get in our positions to start wrestling again. Carlos was on bottom. If I could keep him from standing up, he wouldn't score on me. As soon as the whistle blew, I felt Carlos lunge forward and up, but I held tight and dragged him down to the mat. He was face down and scrambling to get out from under me. I needed to turn him, then pin him.

I snaked my hand around his neck and tried to reach across his chest to pull him into a cradle. If I could just lift his leg, I could force his upper back into the mat. But just as I began to move his leg up toward his face with my other arm, I heard Carlos snicker and whisper, "I remember this." The referee didn't hear him above the cheering.

Suddenly, I was back on the girls' bathroom floor. I could see Zonta up against the wall with wide eyes staring at us. I pushed the image out of my head. "Shut up."

Then I felt his nails on my arm again. My wounds had mostly healed. Since I didn't have any oozing wounds, I hadn't covered them.

But I wished I had, because Carlos quickly drew blood again. The referee blew the whistle, and I had to let go of Carlos again. I felt panic begin to rise. I had to remind myself that this was different. This was wrestling. There were rules. I was safe. I waited for the penalty call, but instead, the ref looked at my arm. "Were those wounds there before the match?"

My mouth dropped. "Well . . . yes. I mean, no." I felt myself take too deep breaths. I had to calm down. The referee waved for me to follow him to talk to Coach.

"Coach Miller, were these wounds previous injuries?" The ref asked again.

Coach didn't hesitate. "Yes, but they were healed. They should not have opened so easily unless the other wrestler forced it to happen."

The referee shook his head. "There is no way to prove that. Since they were there before the match, it is up to you to deal with the blood and wound now. As soon as you are ready, we will continue."

"But . . ." I started to argue. Coach quickly grabbed my shoulder and moved me to the far end of the bleachers, where the athletic trainer on-site could clean up my blood and bandage my arm. The stinging on my forearm finally hit me. I took deep breaths, trying to push away the reality of what had just happened.

"Blake." Coach tried to sound calm, but even his bald head was turning red. "Look, I don't know what his end game is, but you have to find a way to end this before he does anything really serious to you."

"But if he really hurts me, he'll be kicked out." I pointed out the facts. The athletic trainer ignored us as she continued to bandage me up.

"But he wants to be kicked out." Hunter's voice was right behind me. I hadn't realized how close we were to Gavin and Hunter. I turned and saw that Hunter and Gavin had scooted in behind me.

"What?" Coach raised his voice.

This time Gavin spoke. "He didn't tell us, I swear."

"Then what makes you say that now?"

Gavin swallowed. "He *did* tell us that he wants to make it so Blake won't get very far. But . . . we didn't know until right now that he plans to injure him."

"Play dirty," Hunter added. "Not cool."

I didn't know what to think of these two. Gavin had been so *not-cool* for almost two weeks. I didn't feel much like trusting their word on anything. I glanced briefly at the two of them. "Not sure I can believe a word you're saying. For all I know, you're just trying to get in my head and freak me out." I looked at Coach, waiting for him to say something, but he didn't. He just nodded. Gavin and Hunter suddenly frowned and leaned back. If I was right, their body language seemed to say they were surprised at my response. Either that, or they both had an upset stomach at the same time, which was not very likely.

"Done," the athletic trainer said and then nodded to the ref.

I was expected to return to the match. If I didn't, I would have to forfeit the match and not move on to the next round. If I went back, I would for sure face another one of Carlos's tricks. He didn't care about anything but taking me down. He had nothing to lose. I was screwed.

Chapter 39

Calm

We hadn't even finished the first period. We only had thirty seconds left. I had a choice to make. End it now or drag this on for two more periods. I didn't know how I was going to do it. I took three deep breaths and felt my panic simmer down.

This time I started on bottom. I knew I could stand up and get away to gain points. But it wasn't about points anymore. I took my time placing my hands on the mat in front of me. I nodded that I was ready for Carlos to come in behind me. He placed one hand on the back of my elbow and then reached around to hover his other hand over my navel. As soon as the whistle blew, I jumped up and turned to face him. Within seconds we were leaning into each other, head-to-head with our arms stretched out, trying to get a grip on the other one. We had our arms locked. As soon as the whistle blew for the end of the period, Carlos let his hand slip down to my bandage and squeezed my injury. I flinched and jumped back. The referee didn't see it, but others in the crowd did. A few people yelled, "Unnecessary roughness!" and, "Booo."

I was confused. I didn't understand how wrestling worked anymore. Were there rules or not? I didn't even know what to think, so I looked at Coach. He was fuming. "Ref! Pay attention. Will you? That was a penalty!" The referee ignored him as Tank went up to Coach and tried to calm him down. We didn't need a technical penalty given to our team because of Coach. Coach nodded at Tank and then focused on me as I moved back into the middle of the mat for period two. "You take him down now. You *know* what to do! DO IT!"

I looked at Carlos's back as he placed himself on the mat. On all fours with his back to me, he looked so innocent. He felt safe and trusted me. He trusted me to follow the rules. He had nothing to fear. He counted on that. The ref signaled for me to move in behind Carlos. I did.

The whistle blew, and before Carlos could stand up, I reached my right hand down to grab his right ankle. I pulled it up, forcing him to fall forward, with me still on his back. He reached his left arm back and clasped my left forearm. I felt pain shoot through my arm, but the whistle did not blow. I remembered Coach telling me I could wrestle if I didn't have an issue with the holds that would put pressure on the scratches. I had told him it wasn't a problem. I had been so sure. I told myself this was just a hold, nothing else. I gritted my teeth and pushed through the pain. I could hear the crowd booing, even if it was legal.

At that moment, I realized Carlos wasn't even trying to change positions. He was just digging in deeper and deeper. I'd had enough. I quickly backed off and jumped up. I had to try to pin him from a different angle. Carlos jumped up too and faced me. But his eyes suddenly looked over my shoulders, and he frowned. I didn't dare look behind me. I was sure it was a trick to take me down.

We circled the mat, with Carlos's eyes glancing toward my team's side of the mat. I still didn't look. Suddenly, I heard Gavin yell, "Blake, you take down this Hemby Hawk backstabbing traitor!"

Then Hunter's voice finished with, "You are Hancock Thunder. Strike and strike hard!"

I turned my head to see Gavin and Hunter flanking Coach's left side and Tank and Owen on his right.

I quickly looked back at Carlos. For the first time during the match, his eyes narrowed, and he flexed his jaw. I knew what that meant. He was pissed. The more pissed he looked, the calmer I felt. Coach had told me a long time ago that I was a good wrestler because I was a wrestler who used logic, not emotions. I knew what to do. I didn't just understand the rules. I understood every detail of every move and when and how to use them. That was what Coach had been trying to tell me all along! At that moment, I knew Carlos had lost his edge over me.

Suddenly, I heard Tank yell, "PUT OUT THAT FIRE!"

I knew exactly what Tank was telling me to do. I didn't have to think. I let my wrestling calm settle in, and then I struck. I moved in fast and grabbed both of Carlos's biceps. Then I let go of his right arm and dropped to my knees. At the same moment, I tucked my head, pulling his left bicep in tight over my shoulder as my right arm slung through Carlos's legs. With Carlos slung across my shoulders, I quickly popped him up in the air, still holding his left bicep. His feet shot straight up as his whole body rolled over the top of me, landing on his back. Still holding his arm down, I leaned my head back, twisted my body, and shoved my whole weight on top of him. I pinned him in seconds. It was a perfect fireman's carry.

As I stood up, I looked at my team and nodded. They were jumping up and down. Carlos walked off the mat without shaking my hand. That was okay with me. My whole team cheered, and others in the gym stared at us. We acted like I had just won first place. And even though I did go on to place first in my weight class that day, it was the first match that my teammates and I celebrated the most.

Chapter 40

Worth It

I felt the weight of each jar of jelly as I lifted it onto the shelf. I couldn't remember the last time I had been so sore after a tournament. I was always sore but never this bad. This time it felt like I was lifting bricks and not jars.

"Moving slow today, Champ?" Lilly was pushing a cart full of boxes of candy. She stopped a few feet away from me. The candy aisle was across from the jelly.

"Yeah. It was pretty intense." I touched the new bandage on my arm before I lifted another jar onto the shelf.

"Was it worth it?" Lilly asked as she opened a box and pulled out some bags of jellybeans.

Worth it. No one had ever asked if something was worth it. "I guess so . . . I mean . . . I won, right?"

Lilly shoved the jelly beans onto their hooks before she turned to face me. I looked down at the next box of jelly. "Sounds like you're not so sure." But I *was* pretty sure. It felt good that I had won. Was something wrong with that? Had I said something wrong, again? So I just reached for another jar. When I didn't answer, she added, "I mean, I think it was worth it. From what I hear, you finally put Carlos in his place."

I looked at her and frowned. "But you made it sound like I shouldn't think it was worth it."

Lilly grabbed another bag of candy. "I didn't mean it to sound that way. I just wanted to make sure *you* thought it was worth it too." She shoved the candy onto a hook.

A heavy-set woman squeezed between us and grabbed a jar of jelly. One that I had just set neatly into place. I took a deep breath. I always had to remind myself that that was what was supposed to happen. It meant I was doing the job right. It did *not* mean she was messing up my system. After she walked away, I quickly put another jar in that empty space. I looked at Lilly again. "It *was* worth it to me."

Lilly looked up from her box of candy and smiled. "Good." I looked away as she added, "Life's too short to guess if something is worth it or not."

"Is it worth it to you?" I asked, suddenly curious.

"I just told you it was—"

"*Not* me winning." I grabbed a jar and moved it back and forth between both hands. I didn't look at her as I asked, "I mean . . . is it worth being hungry and not asking for help?"

I moved the jar back and forth a few more times before I looked at Lilly. She was quiet. She was looking at the bag of jelly beans. "I don't know yet." She lifted her eyes to the wall of hooks already filled with gummy worms and hard candy. "I can't help but believe it has to be worth it." She shoved the bag onto a hook and then looked right at me. I saw something in her eyes before I looked away. I had seen that look before. Penny gave Mom that look when she was fighting to get her own way. Mom always said that Penny's strong willpower would get her in trouble one day. Lilly cleared her throat and added, "I'll tell you what, Blake. When I find out, I'll let you know. But for now, I got to keep doing it my way. Okay?"

Willpower. That was all I could think about as I answered, "Okay."

Chapter 41

Sorry

"I heard you won on Saturday." Zonta stopped me in the hall before first period on Monday. She had a huge smile on her face. I didn't know what to say at first. This was the second time in a week that she had stopped me in the hall to talk to me.

I looked down at her feet and shifted to my left side. "Yeah, I did." I nodded.

"That's great!" she said and suddenly touched my arm, the one with the new bandage on it. I quickly pulled away, confused. I looked up, and her smile softened. "I heard what happened . . . you know . . . with *him*." She wouldn't even say Carlos's name. "I'm so sorry."

I touched my arm, but I didn't feel sad or afraid. I felt different. "I'm not."

She frowned. "What?"

"I'm not sorry about what happened during the match," I stated. I had told Lilly it was worth it. I wanted to be clearer than I had been with Lilly at first. I wanted to make sure Zonta saw I had no regrets. I pushed down the edges of the bandage. "It's finally over. He lost. I won." I looked up at her. "We won."

Her eyes went wide, and she smiled. "I guess you're right." She took a deep breath. "At least for now."

Lilly came up next to Zonta. She had her camo backpack slung over her shoulder. She smiled at Zonta and then looked up at me. "Hey, Blake. What's up?"

"Not much." I threw the phrase back at her, "What's up with you?"

"Not much," She lied with a big smile.

I tried to smile, but Zonta's last comment didn't sit right in my chest. So I asked her, "What do you mean *for now*?"

Lilly didn't move but focused on Zonta. Gripping her books to her chest, Zonta lifted her one free hand in the air and explained. "You never know, Blake. Carlos could be up to something. He always has been."

Lilly frowned. "What are you talking—"

"But it doesn't mean *he will*." I needed to make sure I finished talking to Zonta before Lilly started talking about other things. I didn't want to worry about Carlos. I was done with him. I wanted Zonta to know that.

Zonta reached out and touched my bandage again. This time I didn't pull away. "You're right. It doesn't. But I'm not going to bet on it."

Lilly cleared her throat. "Okay, you two." We both turned to face her. I watched her reach out and put her hand on Zonta's shoulder. "Let's talk about something else."

"It's not that easy," Zonta argued.

"No, it's not. You have a right to feel the way you do. I get it! Trust me, I do." I suddenly remembered Lilly coming to school with bruises. I never figured out what that was about, but it made sense that she *got it*, in some way. Lilly wasn't finished. "I know you think about it all the time and that you fear it will happen again. It will start getting better. I promise." I dared to look over at Zonta, who seemed almost frozen, staring at Lilly.

"Is that really what you do?" I asked. Zonta didn't look up at me. Instead, she locked her eyes on Lilly. Lilly didn't say anything, but her face softened up. I looked down at my arm again. I realized for the first time that *my* wounds were visible. *My* scratches would fade. *My* head was already in a better place. For me, it wasn't just about what happened two weeks earlier. It was about how I had changed from who I was *before* the attack. I was stronger. I was not trying to be someone I wasn't anymore. But Zonta? Even though she had no visible bruises or bandages, her injuries would take way longer to heal than mine.

Zonta wiped away a tear before it had a chance to fall. "Oh, well. I—"

"I'm sorry." I blurted out the words without thinking. But it seemed the right thing to say. Something in me needed to say those words to Zonta again.

Zonta looked up at me. I tried to hold eye contact, but I stared at the tears that Zonta couldn't stop from rolling down her cheeks. "What? I already told you—"

"Listen! I'm sorry for what happened. I tried to tell you before, but then you went off on how I was so great and all. But . . . I'm *not* so great. I . . . I should have stopped it earlier. If I had just figured it out sooner, then you wouldn't be so hurt." I shook my head. "I really wish I could have a do-over."

Zonta wiped her cheeks with the back of her sleeve and handed her books to Lilly. She looked up at me and asked, "May I?" I realized she wanted to hug me. I didn't do hugs well. Except with Penny and Mom. Only because they made me learn. They told me it was important to them. It was their way to show me that they cared about me, even if it didn't mean as much to me. Zonta needed it, so I took a deep breath and nodded. Zonta moved in close and wrapped her arms around me.

She didn't let go as she spoke into my chest. "I'm not upset with you, Blake Dockins. I want you to hear that. I want you to know none of this is your fault."

I reached out my one free arm and patted her shoulder. "It's not your fault either." I heard a small sob, and she hugged me even tighter as I continued to pat her back and take deep breaths.

Suddenly, Lilly flung her book bag onto the floor, along with Zonta's books, and came in to embrace both of us. "Group hug!"

That was too much for me. I quickly backed up, and Zonta let go, shoving Lilly. "You had to!" Zonta teased. But she only managed a small smile. She wiped away her tears and then reached down to pick up her books off the floor.

Lilly picked up her book bag and smiled. "Couldn't let you have all the fun." Lilly glanced at me for a second. I wasn't sure what she was thinking, but her smile faded, and a serious look crossed her face. She quickly shook it off and forced a smile. "Don't want to miss out anymore."

Still smiling, Zonta shoved Lilly's shoulder again. "What are you missing out on? You're the one having all the fun! You're your own woman! You have nothing to fuss about."

Lilly nodded. "My own woman!" She looked at me and nodded. "Yes. That's what I am." It was pretty clear to me, but Lilly, knowing I didn't always get everything, added, "I get to make my own rules. Make my own choices. You're right, Zonta. I have nothing to fuss about."

Even though I knew Lilly was trying to tell me she was okay on her own, I wondered if she really was. Still, as I watched Zonta and Lilly tease each other, I knew Lilly was not really alone.

Zonta caught me staring at the two of them as they kept on with their strange way of showing friendship. She nodded at me. "Thanks."

I smiled back at her. "Same."

"What about me?" Lilly added.

Zonta looped her arm through Lilly's and dragged her into first period. I shook my head as I followed them.

Chapter 42

Just Nice

I sat down at my desk and was surprised to find Mateo scooting himself around in his seat to face me. He pulled out one of his earbuds and reached out his fist. "Nice job!"

I fist-bumped him and smiled. "Thanks." I couldn't believe it. He rarely spoke to me. I wondered if he was a possible friend too. But just as quickly as he faced me, he turned back around, shoved his earbud back in his ear, and was done with me. I was okay with that. He had always made it clear that he couldn't stand me. Maybe this meant he could at least put up with me for the rest of the year.

"Hey, Blake!" Ozzie yelled from his seat. "Heard you took out Carlos AND won first place. Congrats!"

"Thanks." I smiled. But just as I was going to say something else to Ozzie, a body moved in between us.

"Hi, Blake." Emma was standing in front of me.

I looked up at her. "Hey." I smiled at the dark blue lowlights she had added to her jet-black hair. "Like your hair."

She twisted a part of the long blue strands around one finger. "Thanks. Mom was pretty pissed."

"I bet."

"So." Emma was still looking at me. "See you at lunch?"

"Sure," I answered back. Had she just asked me to sit with her at lunch?

She smiled. "Great." And then she quickly moved to her seat. I had never realized before how pretty her dark eyes were. Then I realized why. That was the first time I had held eye contact with Emma. I had only ever kept eye contact with Mom and Penny. I trusted them and knew they got me. Did that mean Emma got me? I looked over at her and then quickly away. I didn't want to freak her out and stare at her. I scared away Chastity that way. I thought she liked me too, but when I stared at her all the time, she started calling me a freak. I hadn't really talked to Chastity since she and Owen Hemby started dating. At least that's what I thought they were doing.

I glanced back in Ozzie's direction and saw him staring at me. Grinning. He gave me a thumbs up and nodded his head at Emma. Did he think that I liked Emma? Could he see that on my face? I had to stop being so obvious.

I didn't look in Emma's direction again for the rest of the class period. I didn't want to obsess over what had just happened. I had to tell myself that she was just being nice, nothing else.

Chapter 43

Fireman

I felt like I was walking into the caf for the first time. I sort of knew where Emma sat, but I didn't want to walk over to her and her friends and feel stupid if they didn't want me to sit with them. What if Emma only meant she would *see* me at lunch, not *sit* with me at lunch? I held my tray of food for at least a full minute.

"Blake!" Gavin yelled. I turned my head and saw Gavin, Owen, Hunter, and Tank all sitting at the table with Ozzie. Ozzie didn't seem too happy. Even though he had congratulated me earlier, he had no idea what had happened on Saturday with the guys.

Gavin waved for me to join them. I walked over to the lunch table. *My* lunch table. I stared down at the guys. Tank and Ozzie were my friends, but I still wasn't too sure about the other three. I knew Gavin, Owen, and Hunter were trying to make up for pushing me away. That meant something. I felt a part of me relax. Maybe I wasn't someone they would cancel again so easily. "Aren't you going to sit down?" Owen asked.

"I wouldn't," Ozzie said as he looked at the guys with disgust. "After the way you've treated him." He pulled off his Browns cap and placed it next to his tray. He kept messing with his cap and didn't look at the guys around him again.

Gavin's eyes widened, and he looked at me. "Tell Ozzie we're all good. Will you? Otherwise, he might kill us with his attitude."

I looked at Ozzie, who had stopped messing with his cap and was holding a burger halfway up to his mouth. I dropped my eyes. "Yes. We're all good." I nodded, although it was more like getting-there-good.

"Seriously?" Ozzie shook his head. "Just like that?"

Gavin slapped Ozzie's shoulder. "See, I told you."

"I swear, boy, if you touch me again!" Ozzie stared at Gavin's hand as the former football captain lifted his hand off of Ozzie. He looked at me and then at the guys. He put his burger down on his tray, shoved his Browns cap back on his head, and stood up. "Look. I don't know what happened to make it all right. But it's going to take me *way* longer than a weekend." He nodded at me. "Happy for you, Blake." Ozzie turned and slowly carried his tray across the caf. It didn't take long for Zonta to notice and wave for him to join her table, where Lilly was sitting along with several freshmen.

"How does it feel to be going into Regionals with a conference win?" Tank grinned at me.

Still standing with my tray, I smiled back. "I don't know, you tell me?" Tank had also come in first in his weight class, which was expected.

"Sweeeeet!" Tank started singing and stood up to do a very intense victory dance. His large size did not keep him from missing a beat. Everyone around started laughing and cheering.

"Blake?" Emma came up next to me as everyone was still watching Tank. "Are you waiting for me?" I looked at my tray and nodded. I guess I had been. She bit her lip gently and then smiled. "Great. Come on. I have some people I want you to meet." She started to walk away and I began to follow.

"Hey, Blake. Where are you going?" Hunter asked. I stopped and looked back at him. The rest of the table settled down and looked at me too.

I looked toward Emma, who had stopped. She was waiting for me. I glanced back at my old table. "Emma asked me to sit with her."

Gavin raised his eyebrows and smiled. "Oooohh. You going to get you some eggroll—?"

"Shut up, Gavin!" I said before he could finish his statement.

Tank punched Gavin's shoulder. "You've been shut down! Don't mess with the Fireman!" They all laughed. *Fireman.* I guess I had a new nickname. I was okay with that. "Go on, Fireman. See you at practice."

And that was it. The guys started teasing each other and laughing. Adam and a few other younger wrestlers came up to join the table.

I turned and followed Emma.

Chapter 44

Friends

I sat down next to Emma as she scooted in across from a tall, skinny, white boy with curly brown hair that reached his shoulders. I recognized his face but didn't know his name. Suddenly, I wondered if it was Emma's boyfriend. He smiled at her, and I frowned. He glanced at me, and his smile dropped. "Why is he frowning at me?" The boy asked. "I thought you said he would play nice." He looked at me again, and I looked down at my tray. I should have grabbed something besides a burger. It was going to be cold.

I felt Emma shove my shoulder. I didn't move away. "Blake, why are you frowning? You haven't even met Billy yet."

I shook my head. "I don't know." I glanced up. "Sorry, man."

Billy threw his arm out at me across the table to shake my hand. "Let's make it official. Hi, Blake. I'm Billy Seaberg! Nice to meet you!" As I shook his hand, he rolled his eyes dramatically. "I think."

Seaberg. Billy. My eyes widened. "Oh, I know you!" I had flashbacks to my first two years at Hancock High. They weren't memories I was proud of. I dropped his hand and looked at my burger again. I remembered being a jerk to Billy or at least joining in on the trash talk behind his back. Suddenly I felt that guilt. That knowing that I had been wrong.

"What's the matter?" Emma nudged me again. I shook my head. It had been a mistake to sit with Emma and Billy. Who else would come to sit with us? "Come on, Blake. Billy is my best friend. He won't bite."

"Not unless you want me to?" Billy teased.

"Billy!" Emma fussed at him.

"I'm sorry." I blurted out. I still hadn't touched my burger. If I said something, maybe the guilt would go away.

"Okay." Billy laughed. "I knew he was different, Emma, but come on."

"You're gay. Right?" I glanced up for a second.

Billy put his hand to his cheek for a second and then held it out. "Well, duh."

Emma leaned in close to me. "What's wrong?"

"I said I'm sorry." I looked at her. What didn't they understand?

"Okay, Blake. You're sorry." Emma was calm. "But for what?"

"For all the stuff we said . . . I said . . . about Billy. Over the years." I looked away again and took a deep breath. "I didn't mean to hurt you."

Silence. I finally looked up and saw Billy and Emma staring at me. Billy suddenly broke out into laughter. "Emma. You're right. He'll be a lot of fun."

"What?" I was confused. "Why aren't you mad at me?"

Billy took a sip of his bottled water. "Look, Blake. I never heard those awful things. And if I did? Well, there is more where that came from. I don't really give a rat's ass what people say about me." He pointed at himself with both of his hands. "Take me or leave me. That's all there is to it."

"But—"

"Are you going to eat that?" Imani plopped down across from me.

I grabbed my burger off my tray before she could touch it. "Yes."

"Too bad. I could use a second burger." She smiled. "Looks like you're moving outside of your safety zone."

A few weeks earlier, I might have argued with Imani. But she was right. She was always right. "I guess so."

Emma knocked my arm again. She was doing that a whole lot. "Let's be real. I got him to do it." When I looked at her, she was grinning. I felt something inside me lift. I felt . . . happy. I glanced at Billy. He seemed happy too. Imani had broken off Billy's explanation, but he seemed okay with moving on. I had a feeling that those moments of guilt weren't over for me. But I hoped there were more people like Billy, who didn't let jerks like me get to them.

Imani waved at a few of her other friends to join us. Before I knew it the table was full of people I recognized but never knew before. One girl was named Summer and the other Mary Ann. They all started talking about a bunch of things I knew nothing about. But at one point, Imani started talking about maybe one day working for the Red Cross.

Before I knew it, I spoke up. "Do you know that the Red Cross flag came from the Swiss flag?"

"Really?" Imani looked at me.

I could still hear Mom's voice telling me to stay quiet and never share my obsession with flags, but Kyle had said I should. That people would want to know. If I was reading Imani's face right, then Kyle was telling me the truth. "Yes." I didn't stop. "So this guy who came from Switzerland started the Red Cross back in 1863. They decided to take the Swiss flag, which is all red with a white cross, and flip the colors."

"Wow. How do you know that?" Billy leaned across the table.

"I know a lot about flags . . . All flags." I looked from face to face, trying to figure out if they thought I was a freak or not. But all I saw was something that looked to me like curiosity.

"Seriously?" Billy added. He started thinking. "Okay . . . tell me about . . . the Mexican flag?" And I did.

They grilled me with ten more flags before they went on to new topics. But I was okay with that.

I caught Emma staring at me, which made my stomach flip. I smiled at her, and then she slammed me with that huge, beautiful grin. I wondered if it meant she liked me like I liked her. But Mom's voice in my head was louder, reminding me that a girl being nice to me didn't mean she wanted to be my girlfriend. I didn't want to lose her as a friend, so I had to put my feelings in check.

As I sat there and listened to the chatter and enjoyed Emma's smiles, I finally had a chance to take a bite of my burger. It was cold. But I didn't care.

Chapter 45

New

"I have a new favorite," I said to Penny as she jumped up onto my bed. She snuggled next to me, and we both looked up at my ceiling.

"Which one?" she asked.

"Kiribati." I pointed at the flag that was lined up in the middle, furthest to the right. There was no more room between it and the wall.

"Oh, that one *is* pretty." She snuggled in closer. "Do you like it because it has waves and a golden sun? Does it make you wish you were on a Pacific Island instead of here in this nasty cold weather?"

The weather had been cold, even though it hadn't snowed. It was the middle of February, and I had placed second at Regionals. Tank had placed first, again, in his weight class. This coming weekend, he and I would head to the state wrestling finals. We were ready. Mom hadn't made it to Regionals, but she promised me she'd be at State. I wasn't counting on it. But I wasn't upset with her either. I knew that she was working hard so I could wrestle in the first place, so I didn't have to spend every day after school working at Food Time Grocery. I was thankful.

The last two weeks since I had wrestled Carlos had flown by. Nothing much had happened, except that I still ate with Emma and her friends. I guessed that Emma *was* just being nice, and I had to work on not staring at her too much. I was happy she didn't seem to mind when she caught me. Then there were those moments when she stared at me, or winked at me, or even touched my arm when I let her. I guessed that maybe some friends did that to each other, although I didn't see anyone else doing it. But I kept telling myself that it was at least good that she didn't hate me anymore. That had to be enough.

Ozzie still ate with Lilly and Zonta. Imani, Summer, and Mary Ann sat with them half the time and with us the other half. Weird really. I didn't know what the deal was between Emma and Zonta, but since no one said anything, I never asked. But Ozzie, Zonta, and Lilly always talked to me in class and in the halls. Wrestling practices had been great, and everyone was cheering on Tank and me.

Mom hadn't pushed me anymore to "be normal" by following her rules. Not because her mind had changed, but because she saw how much better I was. I had been calmer. I felt it too. Kyle would look at Mom once in a while, and he even said, "I told you so," a few times. But he finally stopped after Mom looked like she was about to cry. I hugged Mom that day. She was surprised. I had never gone in to give her a hug before, but it seemed like she needed it. I patted her and hoped it was a good enough hug. I was pretty sure I did something right since Kyle was grinning from ear to ear.

As we looked up at the flags that day, I shook my head at Penny. "Nope." I smiled at her. "How did you know Kiribati is in the Pacific Ocean?"

Penny stuck out her chin. "Well, for your information, you're not the only smart one here!"

I laughed. "Right. I'm sure I told you at some point."

"Maybe." She giggled. "Go on. Tell me why it's your favorite."

I gazed up at the flag. Blue and white waves reached across the bottom half while the top's red horizon had a flaming gold sun reaching up out of the sea. Above the sun flew a golden bird. "I love it because it shows action."

"What?" Penny frowned.

"Action. You know? Like there's movement. Something's happening." I knew the bird symbolized power, strength, and freedom. But that wasn't it *at all* for me.

"I see it!" Penny giggled. "Like the sun is rising. Right? And the waves keep changing between the blue and the white? Right?"

"That's part of it. But for me, it's the bird. The bird is flying somewhere," I explained.

"But where?" she asked.

I smiled. "It doesn't really matter. He's just moving on."

Acknowledgements

Writing Blake could never have happened without the help of the following individuals who played a role in the process. I am forever grateful for the time and support you provided. Your engagement in the story and responses to the characters inspire me to continue on this journey into the world of Hancock High.

To my parents Jonlyn and G. Keith Parker, who were willing to take on the first read-through of the manuscript and multiple additional drafts. They have not only embraced the characters' lives with gusto, but they have shown unwavering support for the whole writing process. To Ben Onachila, who also was willing to take on the first read-through and provide me with refreshing feedback. His uncanny poetic ability has helped me iron out some rough edges. To my daughters, Maya Borhaug and Sarah Borhaug, whose read-throughs helped me keep the story and characters real. To Kym Sebranek, Sheila Mooney, Jose Rene Perez, Michael Bower, Shutao Wang, Mary Ann Galyon and Dr. Tara P. Bacote for reading through the manuscript and providing valuable feedback, each bringing their unique perspective to the table, supporting my desire to provide an authentic story. To Nastia Parker for not only reading through the manuscript but guiding me through the intricate world of social media and texting trends.

Thanks to Lukas Sebranek, for his honest insight into how the world is viewed from someone on the spectrum.

Brevard North Carolina's former Police Chief, Phil Harris, for details on police procedure and terminology. Thank you to Beth Branagan, for her insight into teen homelessness. For direction and guidance concerning wrestling I would like to thank Vernon Bryson, Jimmy Jones, Hayden Davis Hooper, and Carlo Colombo. A special thanks to Elijah Eubanks for reviewing and editing wrestling sections.

A special thanks to Transylvania County Schools and Brevard High School for the use of their property for the cover shot.

My daughter, Amy Borhaug, who whispers words of perseverance and courage. Nioca Robinson, whose encouragement I dearly value. My copy editor Julie Overpeck, who not only understands the importance of Hi-Lo books, but helped turn out a professional product.

Sarah Borhaug's time, commitment, creativity and professional skill in shooting, editing and designing the cover are deeply appreciated.

Last but not least, my husband, Tore, for his unwavering support and his steady grounding. Without him, none of it would be possible.

Blake's Text/Slang/Terms

The following are definitions for terms used in *Blake.* Some terms may have other definitions that are not included in this mini-glossary.

2—to, too, two

53X—Sex

athletic trainer—people who have medical skills to manage athletes' injuries at sports events

b—be

counting the lights—in wrestling, when someone is knocked on their back and looks up at the ceiling lights

cradle—in wrestling, a move where the wrestler grabs one arm around their opponent's neck, while looping their other arm under the opponent's knee. The goal is to bring both hands together, which causes the opponent's leg to move up and one arm to be trapped. There are many versions.

double leg—in wrestling, a move where a wrestler who faces their opponent moves in to grab the opponent's two legs and then forces them to the ground

fireman's carry—in wrestling, when the wrestler moves in to their opponent and manages to roll them over their shoulder and land the opponent with their back against the mat

headgear—ear protection that wraps over the head and under the chin

match—when two wrestlers wrestle each other in a competition

meet—when two or more wrestling teams gather to compete

mouth guard—a piece of plastic that fits into the mouth to protect the teeth and tongue

omg—oh my gosh/God/goodness

peeps—people

period—two minutes in a wrestling match

pinned—a wrestling move when both shoulders or shoulder blades are held to the floor mat for 2 seconds

plz—please

r—are

rager—big party

restraining order—a legal document that forces someone to stay away from someone else

reversal—in wrestling, a move where the wrestler, who is on the bottom, quickly moves to be on the top. This move will earn the wrestler points.

seeded—in wrestling, how a wrestler is ranked based on their season's record to determine how they are placed on a bracket for competition

shook up—really upset

sick—1. awful 2. awesome/cool

singlet—a tight, one-piece, stretchy uniform for wrestling

sux—sucks

throw shade—make a rude comment

tri—in wrestling, a meet where three teams come together to compete

ttyl—talk to you later

tbh—to be honest

turnt—to be high or drunk

u—you